"You could make a man forget all he'd ever learned of life,"

Gabe said warily. "Your eyes invite a man into your soul."

Her eyes locked with his, Whitney shook her head. *She* was the one drawn inside. "Only you," she confessed, her throat so tight, it hurt to speak.

"Why?" he demanded harshly. "You don't know me."

"Oh, yes," she said, "I do." She realized it was true. Gabe belonged here, just as she did. He'd returned, just as she had. Looking for home. Lost souls, they had found each other.

Finders keepers? she questioned.

The moment lengthened into eternity. Whitney recognized the anguish he so carefully hid, the goodness he locked away, the tenderness he wouldn't admit to.

"Oh, yes," she whispered. "I know you."

Dear Reader,

As Celebration 1000! moves into its third exciting month, Silhouette Romance is pleased to present a very special book from one of your all-time favorite authors, Debbie Macomber! In *The Bachelor Prince,* a handsome prince comes to America in search of a bride to save his country from ruin. But falling for the wrong woman made his duty a struggle. Was loving Hope Jordan worth losing his kingdom?

If you enjoyed Laurie Paige's WILD RIVER books in the Special Edition line, don't miss *A Rogue's Heart,* as Silhouette Romance carries on this series of rough-and-ready men and the women they love.

No celebration would be complete without a FABULOUS FATHER. This month, Gayle Kaye tells the heartwarming story of a five-year-old ballerina-in-the-making who brings her pretty dance teacher and her overprotective dad together for some very private lessons.

Get set for love—and laughter—in two wonderful new books: *Housemates* by Terry Essig and *The Reluctant Hero* by Sandra Paul. And be sure to look for debut author Robin Nicholas's emotional story of a woman who must choose between the man she loves and the town she longs to leave in *The Cowboy and His Lady.*

Next month, the celebration continues with books by beloved authors Annette Broadrick and Elizabeth August. Thanks so much for joining us during this very special event.

Happy reading!

Anne Canadeo
Senior Editor

Please address questions and book requests to:
Reader Service
U.S.: P.O. Box 1325, Buffalo, NY 14269
Canadian: P.O. Box 1050, Niagara Falls, Ont. L2E 7G7

Laurie Paige

A ROGUE'S HEART

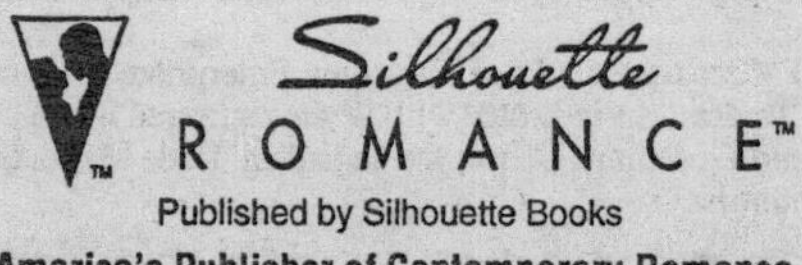

Published by Silhouette Books
America's Publisher of Contemporary Romance

ISBN 0-373-19013-1

A ROGUE'S HEART

This edition published by arrangement with Harlequin Enterprises B.V.

Printed in U.S.A.

Books by Laurie Paige

Silhouette Romance

South of the Sun #296
A Tangle of Rainbows #333
A Season for Butterflies #364
Nothing Lost #382
The Sea at Dawn #398
A Season for Homecoming #727
Home Fires Burning Bright #733
Man from the North Country #772
**Cara's Beloved* #917
**Sally's Beau* #923
**Victoria's Conquest* #933
Caleb's Son #994
†*A Rogue's Heart* #1013

Silhouette Special Edition

Lover's Choice #170
Man Without a Past #755
†*Home for a Wild Heart* #828
†*A Place for Eagles* #839
†*The Way of a Man* #849
†*Wild Is The Wind* #887

Silhouette Desire

Gypsy Enchantment #123
Journey to Desire #195
Misty Splendor #304
Golden Promise #404

*All-American Sweethearts
†Wild River

LAURIE PAIGE

writes: "Sometimes an idea catches the imagination and won't let go. That happened eight years ago when I read about a pair of eagles in a nature magazine. I knew right then that I'd write the 'eagle' story someday. Each time I'd come up with a hero and heroine, I'd wonder, 'Is this the eagle story?' It wasn't until I visited the Rogue River that it all came together—the eagle theme, the story ideas (like a lightning storm my husband and I witnessed there, several stories hit me at once) and the characters. Every part of the river was grist for a story—ranches, logging operations, pear orchards, resorts, towns and fishing villages. It was going to take more than one book to tell them all. And so the Wild River series began...."

A Note from the Author

Now join your hands, and with your hands your hearts. —Henry VI, *Shakespeare.*

Celebrations are special to me. I become quite soggy with happiness at weddings, graduations and birth announcements. I get weepy over anniversaries, puppies and family photo albums (whether I know the family or not).

I am unabashedly sentimental. A hopeless romantic. A dreamer of the first order. A true believer. Love is a force to be reckoned with. Look what happened to all those heroes who scoffed at it and our intrepid heroines!

Naturally I am thrilled to take part in the 1000th book celebration of Silhouette Romance. I can envision readers all over the world joining with me in mutual concern over the fate of Gabe and Whitney, worrying that her love won't be enough, that he won't trust her or listen to his heart, that this chance for a great and lasting love will be lost....

Oh, dear, does anyone have a handkerchief?

Sincerely,

Laurie Paige

Chapter One

"Everything is fine, Mother. We had fresh snow last night, and Moose Creek has a layer of ice over it thick enough to walk on. And the mountains! They're simply beautiful. Remember the last Christmas we spent here with Grandmother? It looks like that, a Christmas card scene come to life. I love it."

Whitney Thompson pressed the telephone to her ear with her left shoulder while she put aside her lists of chores to be done and looked at the items she needed from the hardware store. She'd like to add a jack-of-all-trades to one of her lists. Too bad a person couldn't buy a dependable handyman off the shelf.

Mr. Peters, as cantankerous as his old truck, hadn't arrived yet…for the fourth time in eight days. She glanced at the partially demolished wall of the living room and sighed.

Four days into the new year and already she was behind schedule. At this rate, she'd be lucky to open her bed-and-breakfast inn by January of *next* year.

She stared at the snow-covered mountains visible through the tall windows. To the north, she could see wide white breaks in the fir and pine forest. Those were the ski slopes of the Rogue Mountain Resort.

The ski resort was one reason she thought she could make a go of a B&B. Her grandmother's old Victorian farmhouse—which she'd inherited eight years ago—was on a winding drive right off the county road leading to the expensive but popular resort.

With ten bedrooms upstairs, she planned to accommodate the overflow from the resort, or people who wanted a cheaper place to stay, or perhaps those who preferred a homey atmosphere.

Whitney mulled over names for her place. Rogue River B&B? Moose Creek B&B? Grandma's B&B—

"Did you hear me?"

Her mother's sharp tone interrupted her planning. "Oh, sorry, there was some static on the line. What did you say?"

"Scott got his promotion," Mrs. Thompson said. After a brief pause during which Whitney experienced a strong dose of parental censure directed at her, her mother added, "He's young to make lieutenant colonel."

"I'm glad for him," Whitney said, and meant it.

Scott had been the prime husband candidate out of many that her mother had paraded before Whitney. He was a blond-haired, blue-eyed, broad-shouldered Adonis. Smart, too. A man going places.

Why hadn't she fallen for him? Sometimes she didn't understand herself. It was just...she wanted someone special.

She wondered if she'd recognize this special person...should he ever come along. Her mother had thought she'd found the right man—four times. That fact made Whitney cautious about love. The falling part seemed easy;

it was the staying part that was hard. She wanted a love that would last for all time, like her grandparents had.

"We went to the White House last night—a reception for the new ambassador to the United Nations," her mother said.

Her mother's latest husband, General John G. Jones, had been moved to the Pentagon a few months ago.

Whitney muttered an occasional "Uh-huh" while her mother recited the entire guest list, including each guest's place in society and the clothing of each female.

Relieved to be out of the social maneuvering and politics of the nation's capital, Whitney had no interest at all in returning to that scene. Her mother couldn't seem to grasp the idea. She called weekly to let her headstrong daughter know what she was missing. The strategy didn't work.

A movement across the field caught Whitney's eye. She laid her list aside and leaned toward the window. Her heart speeded up as she peered intently toward the abandoned ranch next door.

Him. Again.

She'd spied the man who'd lingered near the fence between her small acreage and the old Deveraux place last Monday. She'd seen him again yesterday. This was the third time she'd spotted him on her land. He stayed in or near the grove of fir and pine trees, his movements obscured by dark clothing and the deep shadows among the snow-crowned conifers.

A frisson of excitement beat through her.

Her mother finished her description of the reception. "If you come home for Easter, I'll introduce you to several young men you might find interesting..." Her tone indicated that Whitney was hard to please, perhaps impossible.

Whitney's glance went to the tall, shadowy figure among the trees. *She'd already found an interesting man.*

The thought leapt into her mind with the force of a whirlwind. Her heart set up a terrible racket in her chest.

"You could fly home on—"

"Thanks, Mom, but I can't. I have to go now. Tell the general hello for me."

Her mother said goodbye, disappointment in her only child evident in her voice. Whitney hung up with a sigh of relief.

For a moment she drifted in visions of the past. Her mother had tried very hard to make a debutante out of her, the proverbial silk purse out of a sow's ear. A futile endeavor.

Whitney was much too candid with herself and with others to easily fit into the political scene... which involved a lot of posing and posturing as far as she could see.

A Washington reporter had once told her she should apply for a job after she'd sharply questioned a senator regarding a proposed spending bill. That incident had taken place at a party at the senator's mansion in Virginia. Her mother had been furious with her, of course.

She laughed, the sound echoing eerily through the empty, half-demolished room. This was her dream—this old house with all its possibilities. She'd turn it into a home and make her living from it, too. She hoped.

For eight years she'd worked as a media analyst for an important member of congress, saving every spare penny from her salary so she could afford to move here and start her own business.

No one could stop her now!

She stifled another laugh as pleasure shot through her. She felt she was at last living her own life... her *real* life.

Her attention was caught as the man stepped out of the trees. Whitney grabbed the binoculars, a relic of her birdwatching days, and adjusted the focus. The man's face came into view. She studied it, puzzled. She was almost certain she knew him.

Impossible. If she'd ever met him, she'd have remembered.

Yet she couldn't shake the feeling that she'd looked into eyes as dark as night once before. Yeah, in her dreams, maybe.

There was something powerful, something elemental about him that appealed to her—a primitive essence, close to the earth, as if Nature had birthed him in a wild storm of passion. Or grief.

She shook her head at this strange notion.

His face had a forbidding beauty—not handsome, although she found him compellingly attractive—but a visage like that of a lone hunter from long ago. His features were sharply defined, the planes of his face craggy, rising to the thin ridge of his nose and the sensuous perfection of his mouth.

His eyebrows were black, his eyes dark, mysterious pools below them. There were crinkles at the corners.

Not from laughter, she decided, but from staring across vast, harsh distances while he calculated the risks of life. He was a serious man, with a sense of quiet purpose about him. A man with a mission.

Suddenly he froze.

She did, too. Chill bumps caused every hair on her scalp to stand at attention. Her breath caught in her throat while she waited for something to happen.

With the alert intensity of a wild creature, he swung around to face the old two-story Victorian.

Her heart skipped a beat. Feeling like the heroine in a Hitchcock movie, she watched him survey her house with calculated thoroughness. Did he know she was watching him?

Perhaps the sun was glinting off the binocular lenses. No, it was morning, the sun was to the east of the house and he was on the west side. But he seemed to know she was there.

His gaze stopped at the window where she stood. She didn't dare move. She was mesmerized, ensnared... terrified.

At last he turned away, toward the derelict ranch, and she could breathe once more.

A rogue, she thought, with a rogue's instincts, wild and free and dangerous. She suddenly wondered what it would be like to be his mate, to join with him in ancient rites, to come to him under the full moon and fulfill a destiny only dimly understood.

He disappeared. In a blink. Like a dream.

She moved the binoculars back and forth, but saw nothing. She lowered the glasses and surveyed the sparkling landscape that had been glorious in the morning sun but now seemed empty.

A feeling like despair swept over her. She put the binoculars back on the shelf. After stuffing her lists into her jeans' pocket, she put on her parka and grabbed her purse. She had places to go and people to see. There was no time for idle dreaming.

Outside, the snow was flawless, unmarked by human passage. Grimacing, she walked to her pickup truck, marring the landscape's pristine surface.

Once inside the vehicle, a sense of satisfaction stole over her. The truck was new and powerful, with four-wheel drive so she could take on inclement weather and the mountain roads with no problem. She drove the twenty-one miles to the cleared main road without mishap and arrived in town fifteen minutes after that.

"Hello," Mr. Tall called out when she entered the hardware store. He added another log to the Franklin stove, which had belonged to his great-grandfather, brushed his hands together and came toward her. "Come in out of the cold."

Whitney stamped her feet, dislodging the last clinging bits of snow off her boots onto the rug put there for that purpose. She smiled as Mr. Tall welcomed her. She was sure to be one of his best customers before the remodeling was finished.

"Good morning. Mmm, it feels toasty in here. It's really cold this morning."

"Zero degrees on my back porch at 6:00 a.m.," he advised her. "Road open all the way to your place?"

"Yes. The ski resort makes sure of that." She removed the lists from her pocket and selected the one for the hardware store.

Her handyman, Mr. Peters, told her what he needed. She wrote the list, and Mr. Tall supplied the goods. So far it was a simple operation...if she could just keep the old curmudgeon on the job.

Riverton had one grocery, one pharmacy-gift shop, one post office, one gas station-garage, one hardware store, one ranchers' supply outlet plus a couple of cafés and one posh restaurant.

There was one industry in the town, a sawmill started and owned by the same family for five or six generations. All the men in town worked for the mill or the small businesses that catered to the mill families and ranches dotted around the countryside. It was hard to find workers for other projects.

Old Mr. Peters was a retired carpenter, who did part-time work. When he and his truck felt like it.

"Let's see," the store owner murmured, taking the paper and perusing the items. "I think we can fix you right up."

"Good." She went to the stove and warmed her icy fingers.

Mrs. Tall entered from a curtained doorway. Whitney spoke to the plump woman, who had arthritis but continued to knit caps and sweaters for her grandchildren every year.

"Good morning, Whitney," Mrs. Tall greeted her. "Did you have any trouble getting into town?"

"None at all."

"It's supposed to become a blizzard tonight." Mrs. Tall sat in a rocking chair by the stove and picked up her knitting. "I don't know about a single woman living off alone like that."

Whitney thought it kind of the older woman to worry about her, but she'd had enough disapproval of her plans from her parents, including her father and stepmother in Arizona, to last a lifetime. She'd worked long and hard for this chance at her dream. She was going to grab it or die trying!

"My grandmother did it," Whitney said with determined cheer.

"Yes. Abigail Thompson was as independent as they come." Mrs. Tall looked at Whitney. "You favor her, except for being taller and thinner."

Like her grandmother, Whitney had red hair. Where her grandmother's had been a soft, auburn shade falling in deep waves, Whitney's hair was a lighter red with blond streaks at the temples. It flew out around her head in mad abandon, crackling with static electricity when she didn't tame it in a long braid.

Her grandmother had been small and softly rounded. Whitney was five-seven and angular, unable to gain an ounce of weight to add pleasing curves to her figure.

However, she did have a couple of nice features. Her legs were long and shapely, the envy of her friends in school, and her eyes were deeply, darkly blue with lighter streaks in them as if they'd been shot with silver. The blue made them mysterious; the silver made them sparkle. Or so her friends had assured her.

Whitney swallowed as nostalgia brought a tight feeling to her chest. She'd loved Grandmother Thompson, had loved visiting her. The small farm, with its old house and forty acres, had been the one permanent fixture in her life while her mother changed husbands and homes like yesterday's fashions.

"By the bye," Mrs. Tall continued, perling one stitch and knitting the next to form a cuff on the tiny sweater she was making for her newest granddaughter, "have you seen anyone over at the Deveraux place?"

For some reason Whitney felt cautious about mentioning the mysterious stranger. "Has someone bought it?" she asked, evading a direct answer.

"I don't know about that. One of the ranch hands from out that way said he'd seen a light over there two or three times this past week." She paused in her work. "You be careful, hear?"

Whitney nodded. She remembered she hadn't locked the door when she'd left, just in case Mr. Peters got his truck to running and arrived while she was gone.

However, no one could possibly want any of the junk at the house. The good pieces of furniture had been fought over and divided among family members years ago. The remaining stuff wasn't worth anything.

After paying for the nails and supplies, Whitney went to the grocery to stock up on food. The first thing she'd had to purchase for the house was a refrigerator. It had been delivered yesterday, so now she could have fresh food as well as canned.

She counted the money she had left and decided she could afford to splurge on a hearty meal. After treating herself to a big bowl of stew at the café, she returned home.

When she stopped the truck and turned off the motor, she sat there for a minute, her brow puckered into a frown.

Where there had originally been one set of footprints from the porch to the truck, now there were two. The hair prickled on her scalp.

She glanced uneasily toward the woods. The snow was untouched by human or animal tracks in that direction.

Looking in the rearview mirror, she realized someone could have driven to her house in the same grooves as the truck tires. But they hadn't walked in her steps to the porch.

She studied the tracks in the snow.

He—she realized she had assumed it was a man…perhaps her mysterious stranger?—had walked beside her prints, as if comparing the size of her foot to his and the length of her stride to his long step. He'd walked back in his own prints, blurring their size and shape.

As far as she could tell, his prints disappeared where hers did, at the point where she'd stepped into the truck. He must have parked in the same place and gotten out to look around.

Her heart pounded fiercely. Who had been there? And why?

She caught her lower lip between her teeth while she stared at the front door. He hadn't gone up on the porch, so he couldn't possibly be inside. No one but Paul Bunyan could leap from the bottom step to the snow-free area of the porch that she'd shoveled clear that morning.

Her throat went dry. She had no moisture in her mouth to relieve it. Scared? she mocked her quivering courage.

No, she decided.

Her rogue wouldn't hurt her. There was something pure and noble in his manner. Besides, it could have been Mr. Peters. Maybe he'd arrived, gotten out of his old rust bucket of a truck, started for the house, then realized her pickup was gone and had left.

Plucking up her spirits, she opened the truck door and slid out. Immediately she knew no one was around. There was an emptiness of spirit about the house....

She smiled wryly. Next thing she knew, she'd be adding "one friendly house ghost" to her list of household needs so the place wouldn't feel so lonely.

Grabbing a bag in each hand, she hefted her groceries over the side of the truck and ran through the snow with the exuberance of a young deer, grinning at her fantasies.

From the woods, eyes as dark as a moonless night watched as the woman unloaded her supplies. They lingered on long, slender legs and a well-shaped derriere clad in tight jeans, their outline visible when she reached over the truck bed to grab another sack.

"Damn."

The curse went no farther than the whispering of the wind in the next pine.

Whitney laid the book aside and stared into the fire. The wind kicked up a rustle of leaves and pine needles outside. A momentary fear riffled through her at the creaking of the old house, thanks to Mrs. Tall and her concern about Whitney being alone out there in the isolated Victorian.

She was in the back parlor, which was the only room habitable at present. It held all the furniture from her tiny apartment—a bed, night table, chest of drawers, sofa, two chairs and a white ice-cream set, which she'd used as a dining-room table and chairs.

The room also had the only working fireplace, the sole source of heat in the house besides a couple of electric bathroom heaters. Neither the fireplace in the wrecked living room nor the furnace in the creepy basement had been repaired.

She wrapped her arms around herself and shivered as a dog or coyote howled in the distance. The darkness beyond the uncurtained windows seemed tangible, as if she could reach out and touch its obsidian blackness.

An image of the stranger came to her. She could feel his spirit nearby, fierce and protective, yet gentle. It was a comforting fantasy. She smiled and closed her eyes.

If he were here, sitting beside her on the sofa, would he lay aside his book when she did? Would he settle her into the crook of his arm . . . No, he'd lift her and put her on his lap. His smile would be lazy. . . but passionate. His eyes would smolder with love and desire for her, searing her to her soul. He would bend his head slowly, savoring the anticipation, then kiss her.

A board creaked—a loud *pop* of relieved strain. Her eyes flew open. She glanced wildly around the room. All was serene.

She looked out the window. Nothing there but the light from the window falling on the thin, crusty layer of new snow and the trees—

Her breath caught in a gasp. She saw them clearly—footprints leading away from the house and into the woods!

No, it wasn't footprints. It was just the way the light and shadows played upon the terrain . . . and her imagination.

Are you out there? She mentally sent the question across the dangerous darkness to the stranger. *Are you watching over me, or do you mean to harm me*?

She waited, wary and watchful, as if an answer would come out of the night to her.

After a strained moment, she started to pick up the novel, then thought better of it. Maybe she'd better not read any more horror books, even if the writer did make the best-seller lists.

She placed the screen in front of the fire. Feeling rather silly—there couldn't possibly be anyone out there—she took her nightgown into the bathroom to put it on. Having no shades on the windows hadn't bothered her before.

After preparing for bed, she returned to her room, brushed out her hair, rebraided it and slipped between the covers.

With the light out, the fire cast waltzing shadows across the ceiling. She watched them and thought of elegant gentlemen holding beautiful ladies. They danced and twirled, danced and twirled, until she went to sleep.

Whitney ate her breakfast of toast and jelly with her gloves on. The temperature in the kitchen was barely above freezing. Good thing she'd left an electric heater on in there, else the pipes might have frozen and burst during the night.

She yawned, then laughed as her breath plumed in front of her face. If the repairman didn't come to check out the furnace today, she was going to start making voodoo dolls of various people.

The first doll would be for Mr. Peters. He wasn't coming out today, he'd called to say. His shoulder was bothering him.

Why the heck had he said he'd do the job if he didn't want to work? Realizing she was getting upset, she turned her thoughts to other matters. Such as the kitchen.

A glass-fronted oak pantry ran the length of one wall, with a work counter in the center where the pantry had been built around two windows. Under the polished oak counter, the door opened on a kneehole with an electric outlet and a telephone jack in the wall. The space was meant to serve as a desk and kitchen planning area. She'd put a telephone there as soon as she found the extra one, which was still packed, from her apartment.

She chewed on her bottom lip while she surveyed the rest of the room. The tiny, old-fashioned gas stove would have to go.

No! She could use it as a conversation piece in the entrance hall, and it would be useful as a sideboard.

After cleaning up her toast crumbs, she went into the living room and stared glumly at the partially demolished wall. She could wield a crowbar as well as old Mr. Peters. She'd remove the rest of the plaster herself. Wearing a filter over her nose and mouth, she set to work.

Late in the day, she stopped for a cup of hot cocoa. One thing about working—she didn't notice the lack of heat.

Passing a mirror, she grimaced at the white dust all over her. When she took the filter off, her face presented a comical picture.

Her hair was almost all white. She decided she liked that better than red. Maybe when it turned gray, it would be silver like her grandmother's had been.

She washed her face and heated the cocoa. Taking her cup, she went into her living quarters and called the electrician.

Due to the snow, he'd had a couple of emergencies, but he'd be out next week for sure. So he said.

"Right," she said caustically, banging down the receiver after he hung up. She went to the window, afraid her dream was just that...a fantasy that would never happen. She watched moodily as new snow fell from a leaden sky. The beginnings of the predicted blizzard, she assumed.

A dark object near the woods caught her eye.

She leaned closer to the glass and peered intently toward the open space between the pine grove and the fence. Something was there—an irregular lump. A rock? A tree limb that had broken off during the night?

Whatever it was, it would have been covered with snow, which filtered down from a fretful sky, if it had been there very long.

A picture of the stranger came to mind. He'd been wearing jeans, dark boots and a black parka yesterday. A black toboggan hat had covered his hair.

Grabbing the binoculars off the shelf, she trained the glass on the lump. Yes...yes...definitely something that looked like cloth, although she couldn't spot a face.

With an exclamation, she set her binoculars down and dashed for her closet. She changed to heavy socks and insulated boots, jerked on her coat and hat and grabbed a blanket.

She was probably hallucinating, she thought, going out the front door and down the steps, pulling on heavy gloves as she went. But still, if it was a man and he was hurt, she could hardly leave him lying out there with a storm brewing.

The snow was unexpectedly deep in spots, slowing her progress across the rough field. Hidden traps awaited her in the shape of snow-covered shrubs that appeared to be solid ground, then gave under her weight, nearly throwing her. She picked her path more carefully.

Panting, she arrived at the fence, found a broken strand of barbed wire and crawled through the opening. In a few minutes she knelt beside the dark shape.

The man lay face down in the snow, one leg drawn up toward his chest, the other stretched out behind him. His arms were crossed and his hands tucked into his armpits. His posture indicated he'd been aware of the need to keep warm, at least when he lay down or fell down or was knocked down.

Chills chased themselves along Whitney's spine, and she glanced all around, at the woods and fields, to make sure they were alone. They seemed to be.

She looked back at the prone figure. He lay so still. The thought of his death was more than she dared dwell on.

Taking a deep breath to calm her racing heart, she removed a glove and slipped a trembling hand along his neck to search for a pulse. His skin was deathly cold.

She jerked back.

Biting her lip, she tried again. Finding the zipper, she slid it down and slipped her hand into his jacket. Some warmth there, thank God! She found a pulse at the base of his throat, but it didn't seem very strong.

Realizing he needed to be inside as quickly as possible, she proceeded to examine him. Running her hands down his arms, she felt no broken bones. His black knit hat was missing, and she saw blood matted in his dark hair. The wound seemed slight. She examined his arms and ribs.

When she moved down his torso to his legs and ankles, she discovered his foot was caught in an old steel trap hidden in the snow. With an angry exclamation at herself for not noticing this first off, she perused the new problem.

The chain on the trap was attached to a fallen tree limb with a rusty padlock. Damn the barbaric device and the hunters who would use such a thing!

She saw she needed to move the injured man downward a bit to ease the pressure on his foot so she could free his ankle. It could be broken. Should she leave him and call for help?

Afraid to tug on his leg, she wondered if she could move the tree limb. It was large and weighted with snow, but if she could move it a couple of inches, that would give her some slack on the rusty chain....

After brushing the snow off with a stick, she tried tugging on the branch. Too heavy. Spying a rock, she moved it into position where the limb cleared the ground. She wedged the stick in and, using the rock as a leverage point, tried lifting the branch to slide it forward.

That didn't work, but she found she could move the limb by throwing her weight against the stick. She gave several mighty pushes. That relieved the stress on his leg some.

Dropping the stick, she knelt and, putting all her weight into the effort, pushed on the steel jaws of the trap. The spring, brittle with rust, broke. She lifted his foot free.

"Damn it all to hell!"

The jerk of his body and the pained exclamation caused her to drop his foot. The man rolled onto his back, looked at her through glazed eyes, then dropped his head back into the snow, a spasm of pain drawing his lips into a thin line. His hands clenched into fists, but he didn't make another sound.

Whitney leaned forward anxiously. "Can you move? We need to get you to the house." She scooted up beside him.

"We?" he questioned hoarsely. "Who else...?" His voice trailed away. He stared all around, as if pursued by enemies.

Infected by his wariness, she glanced around, too. Nothing between them and the mountains but the wind and the snow. Clouds raced across the sky, indicating more snow to come.

"I'm alone," she told him wryly. "I meant you and I, working together, would accomplish this miracle. Here, I have a blanket. I'll cover you, then go to the house and call for help—"

She started to rise to act on this idea. A fist closed on the front of her parka.

"No," he said.

Chapter Two

His eyes were dark, almost black. Whitney stared into them, startled by his intensity. He looked fierce, dangerous.

"Well, it was just a thought," she said, going very still, suddenly frightened of him, even though he was hurt. Injured beasts were the most dangerous, she remembered reading once.

He studied her, then his grip relaxed slightly.

With a grasp that strong, she decided he wasn't as bad off as she'd feared. "My house is across the field. Can you walk?"

"No." He let her go. "Help me sit up."

She slipped behind him and raised his shoulders, then let him recline against her thighs, his head against her abdomen while he looked around once more. His actions, as if he expected someone to jump from behind a bush, increased her nervousness.

"Drag me," he ordered.

"Can't you crawl?" she countered.

He was a big man. The width of his shoulders was impressive. His thighs had been as hard as marble and thick as an oak when she'd examined him. He was a couple of inches over six feet, she was sure, and at least two hundred pounds, all muscle and bone. Pulling him through the snow would be tough. She feared hurting him more.

"I don't know. I think my feet and legs are frozen."

She made a decision. "All right. Get on the blanket—"

"A blanket," he broke in. He rolled his head to the side so he could look up into her face. "Find a couple of sticks, stout ones. We can make a travois."

He was noticeably weaker by the time she got the sticks and tied the blanket on. After rolling him onto the makeshift gurney, she lifted the poles and gave a heave. The blanket sagged too much to clear the ground. She couldn't budge him.

"Perhaps if I go to the house and get some nails to fasten the blanket, or," she suggested, "I can bring the truck across the field to the fence. If we can get you that far—"

"No. It's . . . too dangerous . . . for you. You don't know where rocks . . . or holes are located."

He was the most negative person she'd ever met. "So what's your idea?" she asked. Noticing sweat popping out on his face, she was immediately contrite. "I'm sorry. Tell me how to help you."

"I'll crawl," he said.

"Take my gloves."

He frowned. "Find mine . . . around here somewhere."

She noticed his speech was becoming slurred as well as choppy. His strength was going. He was hypothermic, in a state of shock, and probably had frostbite. She decided his leg wasn't broken after watching him move it.

Whitney found his gloves near the pine trees and put them on him. While she stood by helplessly, he rose to his right knee and tried to crawl. His left leg dangled behind him. He cursed as he tried to make it work.

"Numb," he finally said. Inch by painful inch, he crept forward. After a few feet, he sank into the snow. "No use."

"Let me try pulling you." She couldn't hurt him any more than he already was, she reasoned. If she didn't get him inside, he would die from exposure.

He ignored her as he rested in the snow.

It took her a few seconds to realize he was unnaturally still. She fought her panic as she searched frantically for a pulse. When she found it, she heaved a ragged sigh. He'd passed out.

She eased him onto the blanket again; then with her hands hooked under his arms, she started walking backward, retracing the path she'd used, his feet and legs dragging through the snow.

She made it to the fence, crawled under and managed to pull him to the other side. Her arms were shaking, and she was panting by the time she stood again.

Snow had gone down the neck of her coat while she'd been on her stomach, pulling him under the fence. She was cold, her hands and face becoming numb. She looked over her shoulder as she started out again, trying to spot the easiest path while dragging her mysterious stranger over the impeding snow.

The field was uphill all the way to the house. If only Mr. Peters would show up.

She stepped into a hole and fell backward, losing her grip on the injured man. She lay there for a second while she regained her breath, but she didn't let herself linger. That was dangerous.

Coming to a decision, she wrapped the stranger in the blanket and rushed across the meadow as fast as she could. At the house, gasping and in pain with a stitch in her side, she tossed her damp parka and sweater aside.

She poured the cocoa into an insulated sports mug, snapped the lid on and set the mug in the microwave oven to heat. Rushing to her room, she changed into a dry turtleneck top and heavy sweater. She raced back to the kitchen, grabbed the mug and truck keys and headed for the door.

He was lying just where she'd left him.

She leapt out, opened both doors of the truck and went to him with the mug of cocoa. After tasting it to make sure the liquid wouldn't burn him, she propped his head against her chest, supporting him with one arm behind his back, and put the spout to his lips.

"Here, drink this," she coaxed. When she got no response, she yelled at him. "Drink!"

He roused without a sound...without even making a startled movement. It was eerie. One minute he was unconscious; the next his eyes blinked open and he seemed fully alert. He glanced at her, then scouted the immediate area, moving only his eyes, before relaxing against her.

Briefly she wondered about a person who had trained himself to do that. Her fingers trembled against the cup. She pressed the plastic spout to his lips. He took a sip.

"More," she commanded when his head dropped back, resting against her chest. A flurry of tingles shot through her, heating her insides. She felt her breast bead into a hard point.

His eyes had closed again, but he was conscious. He turned his head and rubbed his cheek against the hardened tip. The pain-crimped corners of his mouth relaxed a tiny bit.

"Drink," she said, hardly able to speak. A riot was taking place in her body.

He frowned, then gulped the hot liquid down without stopping. He immediately settled against her breast again. Perhaps he wasn't as ill as she'd first thought.

"Now for the hard part," she told him. "You've got to get into the truck."

"Can't."

"Don't talk back." She stood and tugged on his arm. "Come on, up you go." No response. Had he passed out again? She took a deep breath and yelled at him. "Come on, you big ape, I can't carry you!"

"Blasted woman," he growled between clenched teeth.

He glared at her. She glared back. She saw the pain hit him again when his mouth pulled in at the edges, but he didn't make a sound. Using her for leverage, he pulled himself up on one leg.

"Good. Now take a step. The truck is right here." She winced when she watched him try to put weight on his left leg. It wouldn't support him. "Hop," she ordered unsympathetically.

By slow, painful degrees, she got him to the open truck door. Using the last of her strength, she hefted him in and slammed the door before he fell out.

Trembling from the all-out effort, she climbed in the driver's side and drove back up the sloping field to the front door. She looked at the steps wearily.

"Come on. Don't give up yet," she encouraged as she helped him down from the truck. He nearly fell on top of her.

With him hanging on to the banister and her, he made it up the steps. Then he collapsed.

Dragging him again, after what seemed an eternity, she got him down the hall and into her room. There, she stripped off the gloves and his coat, then let him fall back on the bed.

She lifted his feet and removed one boot, but was afraid to touch the other before the doctor saw it.

"Stay there," she said, stripping off the heavy sweater. She slipped a knitted wool vest on over her turtleneck top.

"Where the hell . . . do you think . . . I would go?"

"Ice-skating," she replied, smiling at his tone. If he could come up with cynical remarks, he wasn't going to die within the next few minutes. She went to call the doctor.

"No ambulance available?" she repeated when she spoke to the answering service. She listened as she was told the nearest hospital was in Medford. "That's more than an hour's drive away."

"Let me have your number and I'll have the doctor call you," the cheerful voice suggested.

Whitney left her number.

She hurried back to the sickroom. After tossing kindling into the fireplace, she stirred last night's embers to life, then put on two logs. She placed several towels on the hearth and held one up to the crackling flames. As soon as it was warm, she wrapped it around his right foot.

"Take my other boot off," he ordered.

"I'm waiting for a call from the doctor."

He muttered an imprecation. "Take the boot off."

She leaned over him, testing his temperature with her hand on his forehead. His skin was cold in spite of their efforts in getting him inside. "Your ankle might be broken. I could injure it worse by tugging on it."

Her braid slipped over her shoulder and landed on his chest. He caught it in his big hand. "I'll lose the whole damned foot if circulation isn't restored soon. Take it off!"

Whitney looked into his dark eyes and realized he had a concussion. He must have hit his head on a rock when he was caught in the trap and fell.

New fears shook her jumbled nerves. He could be bleeding internally. With all that jostling around, he might die.

"Be still," she warned, speaking softly as if his concussion were an avalanche she might set off. "You're concussed."

"Tell me... something... I don't know," he said scornfully. His hand tightened on her braid. "Take off—"

"Okay, okay," she agreed, soothing him. She went to the foot of the bed and studied the situation. Without much hope, she tried a gentle tug on his boot. His ankle was swollen. She could see that even with the boot still on. She had an idea.

She removed her snow boots and sat at the end of the bed. Carefully, she slipped her leg between his. Placing her foot into his groin, she found a space beside his... uh... manly parts and braced her foot against him. She noted that he seemed very warm there. A blush heated her face to glowing.

"I—I'm sorry," she stammered when he raised his head from the pillow and gave her a sharp glance, as if wondering at her motives. She grew more flustered. "It's just that... I need something to push against."

One dark eyebrow shot up.

"To... to take your boot off." She groaned mentally. She was acting like a shy virgin in her first affair. Well, after all, a man in her bed was a first. She'd always been particular about things like that. She grinned wryly at the thought.

He let his head fall back. "It's okay, Irish. I won't think you're trying to... ravish me." He paused, then, "Hurry."

She heard the agony he somehow managed to keep from showing on his face. Leaning against the carved footboard, she took hold of his boot by the heel and toe and began easing it off.

"Good... thinking," he whispered. A smile flitted across his lips before they drew together in pain once more.

"Save your strength," she advised. Pushing against him with her foot and keeping a steady pressure on the boot, she felt the leather begin to give. She increased the force and felt the boot slip against his swollen foot. It came flying off.

Against her foot, jammed so intimately against him, she felt the spasm of pain jerk through his body, although no sound escaped his clenched lips. When she tossed the boot to the floor and peered at his face, she knew he was beyond pain, at least for a little while. He'd passed out again. She removed his sock.

The color of his injured foot was that of ice cubes, white with a blue tinge. His toes felt like little chunks of ice attached to a larger chunk.

After a moment's thought, she covered his upper body with the sheet and blankets, then placed both his feet between her thighs. Leaning forward, she pulled her turtleneck out from her body and eased his feet under it, his toes tucked up against her ribs just under her breasts. She wrapped her arms over the sweater and waited for the doctor to call and tell her what to do next.

Whitney jerked out of her doze when her head fell forward. She looked around, startled, then realized she was on her bed with the stranger's feet against her belly.

The sky was dark. Night. She must have slept a long time.

She studied the injured man. He moved his head back and forth, then clenched the blanket in a hard grip. His frown indicated pain, she feared. This was confirmed when he groaned under his breath and shifted restlessly. His lips moved as if his thoughts were troubled. *Delirium*.

Slipping her hands under her sweater, she examined his feet. They were warm. She didn't know how to tell if he'd suffered severe frostbite, but she was very gentle in her examination. She knew the flesh was easily injured in that condition.

As she felt each of his toes, a strange feeling came over her—one of tenderness and closeness. All her earlier misgivings dropped away. She didn't know his name, but he was no longer a stranger to her.

She'd shared an adventure with him, one that wasn't over yet. Now she shared her warmth. In that moment it seemed their lives were destined to intertwine.

"The bond grows," she murmured impulsively, not sure what she meant but feeling profound about it.

Solemn, she watched the flames in the grate. Castles and kingdoms formed, were fought over and won. Knights and ladies rode the galloping flames as they leapt like fiery chargers across the logs. An hour later the ringing of the telephone roused her from her fanciful daydreams. She slipped off the bed.

It was Dr. Payne, whose name she'd found amusing when she'd met him years ago while laid low with the flu on a visit. She explained the problem to him with as many details as she could.

"Can you come right away," she concluded, "or send an ambulance for him?"

"The roads are closed. All the snowplows are over on Interstate 5, trying to keep it open."

She muttered an angry word.

"Sounds to me like you're doing all that can be done," he assured her.

"But he has a head injury, a concussion, I think. He needs help," she pleaded.

"You say it's stopped bleeding?"

"Yes."

"Just keep him still and warm," the doctor advised. "Don't let him on his feet. Keep them elevated and warm, but no pressure on the skin, not even the sheets. Prop the covers up. Call me if anything changes." He gave her his home number. "Get as much warm liquid down him as you can."

After repeating his instructions, she returned to the bedside and stood there, thinking. Finally she took the heated towels from the hearth and put them under his feet, then pulled the sheet and blankets free of the mattress and laid them over the footrail.

In her socks, she padded into the kitchen and returned with two tall plastic canisters. These she placed under the covers, tucked close to the towels. They formed a tent over his feet. It was the best she could come up with at the moment.

Food, she thought. They'd had no supper. She studied his face, relaxed somewhat in sleep. She'd get her shower first, then she'd eat. She would feed him when he woke up.

Later, dressed in fresh clothes, she went to the kitchen, heated some soup and brought it and crackers to the sickroom. She sat in her favorite chair and ate, her eyes on her patient.

Finished, she put the tray aside and wrapped a warm woolen blanket around herself. She raised the footrest of the recliner-rocker and closed her eyes. She couldn't go to sleep. She had to stay alert to keep the fire going and look after the patient.

Gabe opened his eyes and swept the room with a blurry gaze. He didn't move. That was one thing a man in covert intelligence learned fast—don't make any sudden moves; they were a dead giveaway. Very funny, he mocked.

At the moment he felt more than half-dead. And the pounding in his head . . . as if a train were using his skull for a track. His foot hurt, too. He remembered the pain as his ankle was caught in the trap, then falling face down in the snow.

A sigh and a movement alerted him that he wasn't alone. He flicked his gaze to his left.

The woman.

She was curled in an easy chair, a blanket tucked up to her chin. A fire, barely flickering, cast a rosy glow over her.

Not that she needed it. Her hair was fiery red with golden strands in it. Her eyes were blue...the deep, deep blue of the sea around Ireland... in summer... with cornflowers in bloom.

He'd watched her looking at him with her field glasses the other day. Yesterday? He wasn't sure. He didn't know how long he'd been like this... whatever *this* was.

He was pretty sure he had a concussion. How had he gotten it? Oh, yes, the owl and the falling timber...

Stupid...to let himself be surprised...wanted to look over the stolen goods in the barn...lights on the road... hide...quick. So stupid, to be caught like a rookie on his first case. He'd slipped into the old ranch house... his former home... falling down around his ears... literally. An owl had flown at him. He'd dodged. A rotten roof beam had broken loose and fallen.

After that...darkness. He remembered waking and crawling from under the debris... the cold had been excruciating, the pain in his head blinding...needed help...who to trust?

The woman. He'd tried to reach her. His leg... Oh, yes, the trap...the damn bear trap. He'd struggled but... useless...

He'd stared death in the face at that moment. It hadn't been particularly scary. He'd done it before—

The woman sighed again and turned to her side.

He watched her sleep. She'd come to him... in the night, dancing across the snow like a living flame, warming him, taking away the pain... No, that had been hallucination.

He couldn't remember when she'd come to him in reality, prodding him into getting up, making him hurt again. She had yelled and jerked at him until he'd done what she'd wanted, just to get rid of her. He'd only wanted to sleep....

No, that wasn't quite right, either. It was too hard to think...too dangerous not to. He had to expose the thieves...clear his name. Then he'd sell the ranch and leave this place forever.

The redheaded woman stirred, stretched, and lifted her head with a jerk. She glanced around puzzled, not fully realizing where she was. She saw him watching her and went very still.

Then she smiled.

It hit him in the chest, that smile. It curled around inside him like a cat picking the best spot to snooze in. He couldn't remember the last time someone had looked at him like that. Or if anyone ever had.

His mother had loved him. She'd been half Indian, with dark eyes and hair like his. But she'd died. Then he'd only had his father, who'd rarely talked and never smiled.

"Oh," the woman said, "you're awake. And probably hungry."

She rose and busily stirred up the fire until it was blazing once more. He felt the cold receding from the room like an evil spirit before a charm. He smiled. A redheaded charm. *His* redheaded charm. He liked that thought.

When she left the room, he felt the emptiness. When she came back, he was relieved. It wasn't wise to depend on anyone, though. He'd learned that lesson at sixteen, right here at home.

"Here. You need to eat. The doctor said you should have lots of liquids, too."

She placed the tray on the bedside table and bent over him. Slipping her arms under him, she propped him against two fat pillows, then sat beside him. She lifted the bowl and spoon and began to feed him.

To his surprise, he didn't object. He ate the hot tomato soup from her hand, so to speak, as meek as a babe being fed by its mother. Tomorrow he'd do it himself, but for tonight....

"You might have a fever," she murmured, touching his forehead when he finished eating. She shook her head and looked worried. "Drink this. It's an herbal tea. No caffeine. Does your head hurt dreadfully?"

He nodded, then wished he hadn't. It made the pounding worse. To please her, he drank the mild tea down. He didn't like all this TLC. Tomorrow he'd put a stop to it.

She crooned in sympathy and encouragement. It dipped right down inside him, just like her smile. He reached out without thinking and touched her chin. Her skin was pure silk.

Her lower lip trembled, but she remained still.

He had to explore her mouth. Her bottom lip was generously full, the upper one thinner. She had a redhead's complexion—pale skin with rosy cheeks and lips. Her freckles were a golden sprinkle under her skin, not quite visible, not quite hidden.

Like promises of good things to come. He wondered if they were the same over her entire body.

He stroked that trembly lower lip and wished he had the energy to kiss it. He'd like to suck it between his lips and stroke it with his tongue...he wanted to taste her...feel her.

"Soft," he murmured, fascinated. But...it was dangerous to let himself feel like this...foolish....

"You shouldn't. You have to be still," she whispered, a look of wonder in her eyes. She, too, was surprised by the desire, he realized. She felt it the same as he did.

A sense of elation washed over him like a summer rain. She wanted him. The desire was mutual. He sighed in anticipation.

Soon. When he was well.

His energy spent, he dropped his hand from her lips. It landed in her lap, close to the joining of her legs. Her warmth penetrated the material of her jeans and soaked into him. He turned his hand and laid his fingers along her thigh.

She gave a gasp.

The firelight was behind her. Her hair became a fiery nimbus around the perfect oval of her face. "Beautiful," he said, the word torn from him. She was a dream come true.

Alarm jangled through him. He had no time for dreams. He had a job to do—catch whoever was using his ranch as a storage place for stolen goods. This time he wouldn't be falsely accused of being one of the thieves, as he'd been at sixteen. He couldn't afford to be sidetracked by dreams. He knew about those. They never came true.

She left the room with the tray. He checked the windows—no curtains or shades to offer even an illusion of privacy. It made him uneasy. The night could hide a thousand eyes.

When she came back, she brought an electric teapot. "More tea," she explained, plugging in the teapot. "Can you drink another cup?"

"Yes, but first, where's the bathroom?" He could vaguely recall her pouring something hot down him earlier...out in the field...something sweet and hot.

She looked alarmed. "You can't get up," she told him sternly.

"Have to." He pushed the covers off his chest. He still had on his clothes. No wonder he was so damn uncomfortable. He didn't like sleeping in anything, much less damp jeans. "Got to get these off." The effort at moving proved too much. He slumped against the pillows.

"The doctor said you weren't to get up." She stood over him like a guardian angel, her expression fierce.

"Got to get up," he insisted grimly. It was a fact.

Her face brightened. "Wait," she ordered. She hurried out.

He watched the sway of her hips as she left. Those incredibly long legs. He could picture them entwined with his...or clasped around his waist, pulling him deep...

"Here," she said, returning to his bedside. She handed him an old-fashioned milk bottle, a glass one with a narrow neck. Her cheeks wore crimson flags of embarrassment.

He realized what the bottle was for. When he took it, she headed out of the room like a startled gazelle. He wondered at that while he took care of his personal business.

She looked to be in her late twenties, yet she grew nervous over the slightest intimacy or personal matter. She was either shy or inexperienced. Either was hard to believe in this day and age.

He placed the glass container on the floor beside the bed. He'd been injured too many times to be shy about body functions. Doctors and nurses had poked and pried into wounds and cuts more than once in his thirty-two years.

"Okay," he called.

She returned. Carefully avoiding eye contact, she took care of her nursing chores. He heard the flush of water in the bathroom. He was almost asleep when she padded back to his side some minutes later.

"Sit by me," he requested, needing her there.

"How does your head feel?"

"Like heck." He smiled sardonically as he curbed his tongue for her delicate ears. For all he knew, she might have the vocabulary of a longshoreman.

She peered at his temple. "You have blood in your hair. It's dried. The wound is odd, more like you've been grazed by something blunt but hard. There's a lot of bruising. Do you remember if you hit it when you fell?"

"No."

He didn't want to talk about it. With women, he believed, if a man answered one question, they had a dozen more. The less said, the better. He reached for her waist-length braid and felt the soft, curling tendrils at the end. "You have lovely hair."

She blushed again. It was the damnedest thing.

"Thank you." She looked skeptical. "It's awfully red. My paternal grandmother's was auburn. It was beautiful."

Was she putting him on, or did she really have no idea how attractive she was?

He looked her over. She was slender and her breasts were small, but he liked the angular lines of her body. She was strong and fit. He liked that, too. Wimps, male or female, didn't appeal to his tastes. This woman didn't fold in an emergency.

"Thanks for your help today." He wanted to keep her there, her deep blue eyes like twin seas, turbulent with the questions she had about him. She refrained from asking them. He was grateful.

She nodded.

"You saved my life." It gave him a strange feeling to realize it was true. "I owe you for that."

"It was nothing." She looked at him, then away. "You should sleep. It's after midnight."

He caught a flash of some emotion in her and felt the slight hesitation before she spoke. It was very appealing. She wasn't one of those brazen women who assumed they were so attractive a man couldn't resist their charms.

Irish didn't seem to know she had any charms. She did, though. In spades. When he was better, he'd tell her.

"You, too," he told her, remembering she'd slept in the chair earlier. "Go to bed. I'll be okay."

She rose. He let the braid slip through his hand. Pure silk. He hated to let it go. After she built up the fire, she sat down in the chair and pulled the blanket around her.

"I think I'll make it through the night," he said dryly. "Go on to bed."

"Well," she began, oddly hesitant. What was bugging her now? "Uh, maybe later."

He considered the situation. There must be only one bed in the house, and he was in it. Stupid not to have realized this before.

"You can sleep here. I'm safe." He was, but he suddenly wished he weren't. He'd like to do some delicious things to her.

Her eyes opened wide. He'd shocked her. That idea almost shocked him. Had she been raised in a convent?

He tried to smile, to show her he was harmless. He put a hand to his head. "Just don't jostle the bed. My head is killing me."

That drew a smile from her.

"An old excuse, I know," he continued drolly, putting her at ease, talking in spite of his pounding head. "In this case, it happens to be true."

"I sometimes talk in my sleep," she warned.

"I'll answer," he promised. "Come on. I won't sleep unless you get some rest, too."

He watched her struggle with thoughts and emotions too fleeting for him to identify before she made up her mind. "I need to keep the fire going," she said, declining.

He was disappointed, but accepted her decision. He closed his eyes. Sometime later the bed moved slightly as she eased under the covers on the other side. He sighed in satisfaction.

Chapter Three

Whitney stood silently while Dr. Payne examined the patient, who was unconscious or asleep. She wasn't sure which.

She watched the older man's hands as he probed the head wound. Her tension mounted as the doctor frowned, glanced at her, checked the wound, then looked at her again.

"Concussion?" she finally asked, wanting her own diagnosis confirmed. She caught her lower lip between her teeth. The doctor might call an ambulance and take the stranger away. She'd never see him again...

With a start, she realized she didn't want him to leave.

Don't build fantasies out of thin air, she warned her misguided heart. What did she know of this man, except her own wild imaginings?

Her mother had often scolded her for living with her head in the clouds. If she was to make a go of the bed-and-breakfast inn, she had to have her feet planted firmly on the rocky Oregon soil. She had to be a hard-nosed businessperson.

"Mm-hmm," Dr. Payne said. "Did someone hit him on the head?"

"Hit?" Alarm ricocheted through her. "No. I don't know. I assumed he hit his head on a rock when he fell." She leaned around the doctor to run a worried glance over the long, masculine figure that filled her bed.

For the space of a heartbeat, she recalled sleeping beside him during the night. At dawn, she'd risen, washed up and put on fresh jeans and a sweatshirt. He'd never known she was there.

"No, there're wood splinters in the wound. Looks like he got a good lick with a piece of firewood or something. Damned lucky he wasn't killed."

She puzzled over this. "I found him lying in the snow, his foot caught in one of those old bear traps, and thought he'd gotten caught..." She stopped speaking as the implications of the wound hit her. Had someone tried to kill him?

The stranger didn't move until the doctor dug his thumbs into the puffy flesh around the ankle.

The dark eyes flicked open. Seeing the doctor, the injured man relaxed just as quickly as he'd reacted to the pain. He glanced over at her, his gaze resting on her mouth.

"Well, Gabe Deveraux, isn't it?" Dr. Payne inquired, getting on with the examination in spite of the tight-lipped grimace on his patient's face. The patient didn't answer.

Deveraux!

Whitney realized she knew him, in a manner of speaking. She'd been visiting her grandmother when the rancher next door had died. That had been about twelve years ago. The day after the funeral, while she was hiking and exploring the land, she'd come upon a small family cemetery tucked into the woods. A man had stood beside the new grave, his face contorted with a grief so deep it had slashed into her heart.

When he'd seen her watching him, his expression had changed at once. His eyes had narrowed. Sorrow was replaced with a fierce anger. When he'd taken a menacing step toward her, she'd hightailed it out of there, realizing she was on his property and trespassing on his private anguish.

Her grandmother had later told her there'd been bad feelings between the old man and the boy, that the son had left home when he'd been only sixteen. She'd never heard what happened to him.

"Probably nothing good," her grandmother had said. "The boy was involved with a gang of thieves. He was arrested, and then let go for lack of evidence, I think Emma Tall said."

Whitney's heart went out to the teenager who'd run away from an unhappy home. In her mind's eye, she saw the young man who'd come back to bury his father, still not over his anger, yet filled with that terrible, unforgiving grief.

She wondered what kind of life he'd led since then, on his own with no one to care if he lived or died. "If someone hit him and left him for dead..." She mulled over the scant evidence. "Perhaps we should call the sheriff."

"No."

She met the dark, commanding eyes of her patient.

"But if someone is trying to harm you..."

"They're not. It was my own foolishness that landed me in trouble. I went inside the old ranch house, knowing it was ready to fall in. A roof timber crashed down and hit me."

Whitney bit back a reprimand. Naturally he'd want to explore his old home, to relive happier moments there. "But the bear trap, how did you—"

"When I came to, I knew I needed help," he broke in. He sounded as if he resented that fact. "This was the closest place."

He'd been coming to her, she realized. For a moment she stared at him, a thousand questions clamoring inside her.

Dr. Payne released the sore foot. "Lots of contusion, but no permanent injury. Let's see if we can get him out of his clothes."

Her pulse upped its tempo when the doctor suited actions to words and unfastened the jeans.

"Here, I'll lift him. You pull his britches off." Dr. Payne slipped his hands under the patient's hips and lifted.

A tremor of excitement ran through her. She wanted to explore all of him—skin and muscle and sinew, mind and heart and soul. She hesitated, then reached forward to follow the doctor's orders.

"No."

The harshness of his voice startled her. She drew back. He levered his hips up by putting his weight on his right foot. Dr. Payne was able to pull the pants off without help.

The flex of powerful muscles was clearly visible through the thermal long johns as the patient relaxed. The knitted material faithfully delineated every line of his legs and hips.

She was entranced by the perfection of his form. He was a big man, with well-developed muscles on a robust frame. In the woods, he'd moved with the grace of a mountain cat, quick and sure.

His lashes lifted, and he looked directly at her. She saw a wary element in his intent regard, as if he, too, was aware of the deeper currents between them.

Within her own body, needs stirred, leaping like flames upon a fresh log, wild and fiery and demanding. She gripped the end of the bed and fought the fierce impulse of desire.

A special man, she thought, and her heart beat wildly.

Shaken, she murmured an excuse and hurried to the kitchen to put on a pot of coffee. Her hands shook as she performed the task. She worried about her growing obsession with this man, this Gabriel Deveraux, descendant of French fur traders, Native Americans and English colonists.

When she returned to the sickroom, she saw the doctor had removed the outer wool shirt and that the patient wore a thermal shirt underneath.

"I've put a splinted bootie on his left leg to support that ankle while it mends. Do you have a warm sock to put on the right one?" Dr. Payne asked.

"Yes."

"It's a good thing you didn't rub his toes," the doctor continued. "That can cause more damage—breaks the cells open."

"I vaguely remembered that from a first-aid class."

Dr. Payne checked the fastenings on the soft boot that came to the knee. Rigid bars up the sides kept the ankle immobile. "Can you keep him here a few days?"

Her heart gave a giant leap in her chest.

"No need," the patient snapped. He opened his eyes and glared at her, as if she had offended him.

She put another log on the grate, still feeling light-headed with her needs so foreign, yet elemental, that she couldn't define them. She was also hurt at his curt refusal to stay.

He probably had someone else to take care of him. The thought jolted her composure. She stared into the fire.

"Do you have someone to look after you?" Dr. Payne asked in a tone that implied nursing was definitely called for.

Silence greeted the question.

The doctor spoke to her. "Would it be a bother for you to put him up for a while? There's no need for him to be in a hospital, and your place is handy for me."

"It would be no trouble," she murmured, defying the patient's savage frown.

"I'm not staying here."

She met his obstinate gaze without blinking.

"Well, we could send you to the hospital, I guess—"

"No." Their patient vetoed that idea in no uncertain terms. The dark gaze went to the doctor before flicking back to Whitney.

His stare made her weak in the knees, a thing she couldn't remember happening to her in her entire life.

"Hmm," the doctor said. "Then I think you're going to have to stay here."

"I have a room. At the ski resort," he added when Dr. Payne looked skeptical. He raised a hand to his forehead and rubbed it.

Whitney winced when he did. Even talking caused his head to pound. It made hers hurt in sympathy.

Dr. Payne frowned. His experienced hands probed the head wound. "You can't stay alone for the next two or three days."

Gabe glanced at the woman standing at the end of the bed. He couldn't keep his eyes off her, hadn't been able to since he'd spotted her earlier in the week, darting around the old Victorian mansion next to the ranch he'd inherited years ago.

He closed his eyes as pain hit him again, this time from the alcohol old Doc Payne was swabbing on his scalp. The discomfort was of little consequence. He was lucky to be alive.

When he'd come to in the house, he'd been afraid to move, in case the thieves were still around. The night, seemingly endless, was giving way to dawn. He'd known he needed help. He'd climbed from under the fallen timbers, seeking warmth, seeking *her*. Then his foot had been caught. A hell of a lot of bad luck...

The soft, fluting voice of the woman drifted over him as sweet as a caress when she asked the doctor a question.

The woman... she'd been his one piece of good luck.

All his instincts had pulled him in the right direction. He'd longed for her, needed her...and she'd come to him, dressed in flames that warmed but didn't burn. She'd held out her arms, and he'd entered that haven of fire and peace.

That was the last thing he remembered until he'd awakened with the thought that someone was tearing his foot off. When he'd opened his eyes, he'd gazed upon the bluest eyes and reddest hair he'd ever seen.

He bit down on a groan as another pain attacked his head, not the incessant pounding, but a sharp lance that nearly brought him off the bed. Hands caught both of his as he lifted them to stop the torture. Strong, slender fingers linked with his. He knew that touch and relaxed.

The room was blurry, but he no longer saw two of everything. Centered in his view was the redhead, filling his vision like a mirage. Waves of dizziness washed over him. He fought it.

She leaned over him, restraining him while the doctor finished sewing up his head. Her hands felt good, smooth and gentle, small compared to his, but with a strength that was gratifying. She would be a perfect lover.

He wanted her with a rush of desire that was stronger than the pain in his head. Bringing her hand to his mouth, he kissed each knuckle while he devoured her with his eyes.

Bright red surged into her face.

He remembered there was someone else present. "Sorry," he murmured, contrite. He'd have to watch himself. Irish was shy. He'd have to remember that.

"The stitches will leave a neater scar," the doctor said to the woman, putting away his instruments. "I'll stop by tonight on my way home from the office and see how he feels. If I can get through, that is. More snow is predicted. Here, these pills should take the edge off his pain. Give him the antibiotics every four hours. Try to keep him calm and in bed for two or three days." The doctor gave her a humorous grin and handed over several packets of pills.

"I will," she promised, embarrassment riffling her voice like wind on a river, making it soft and shimmery.

Gabe wondered if she would like sleeping under the stars. They could zip their sleeping bags together and watch the night sky. Then he'd make love to her.

"Fine," the doctor said as he closed his bag.

Gabe wished the man would leave. He wanted to be alone with her. He might be concussed, but he wasn't dead, not this time, thanks to her. Had he thanked her for saving his life?

"Thanks," he muttered, remembering how warm she'd been when she'd climbed into bed and... Well, hell, she'd been *intimate* with him...at least he seemed to remember her touching him in a very private place.

A woman didn't do that unless she wanted... Wait a minute, that had been her foot and she'd been trying to take his boot off. Oh, yeah. But then she'd wrapped herself around him...well, around his feet...but he'd thought about how she'd feel if they were touching all over...her skin...so soft and silky...

"Still lots of life left in that boy, so don't worry about him," the doctor advised with a dry chuckle.

"Thank you for stopping by," she said.

Gabe realized her voice was growing fainter, then realized it was him. He didn't want to pass out again, damn it. He saw her walking the doctor toward the door and resented her leaving him.

"I don't think there will be any damage from frostbite, except the skin of his toes will turn dark and peel off."

"Oh. I'd wondered..."

Her lilting voice faded from his hearing as they discussed his case as if he weren't a grown man who'd been on his own for most of his thirty-two years. He heard himself sigh—it seemed he was on the ceiling or somewhere high up, able to hear but not see. He realized his eyes had closed. He was too tired to open them again.

The pain became a plangent booming in the distance. Had the doc given him a shot? He couldn't remember. That was the trouble with being hit on the head. The memory went first. For instance, he couldn't remember the redhead's name...

Irish.

He relaxed. That was it.

Whitney swept up the last of the plaster. She dumped it into the trash bin and sighed wearily. There, the living room looked better without the debris from her demolition efforts littering the floor. While her patient was sleeping, she'd decided to clean up the mess. Now she needed a shower. White dust sifted out of her hair every time she moved her head.

She glanced at her watch. Nearly time for supper. She'd put on a big pot of homemade soup after having tomato soup from a can for lunch. Her patient had refused to eat.

However, he'd roused a couple of times during the afternoon, each time irritably assuring her he was feeling better when she went in to check on him. He was grouchy as well as stubborn as a balky cow.

She tiptoed into the bedroom to retrieve fresh clothes and decided she'd get right into her flannel gown and read in front of the fire for the rest of the evening. Glancing at the sleeping man in her bed, she saw he'd thrown the covers off. He seemed to be resting okay, so she left him alone.

She removed her sneakers and padded into the bathroom in her thick socks. The water was warm, and she scrubbed until she felt silky clean. That was something she wasn't used to—soft water that left her skin as smooth as silk.

After the shower, she wrapped a towel around her hair turban-style and stepped into her gown. She grimaced as she looked into the mirror. With the flannel buttoned to her neck, she did look like a spinster.

She unfastened the top two buttons...then the third. Now she looked like an absentminded spinster who'd forgotten what she was doing in the middle of the job. She slipped the buttons back into place.

A gaping neckline wouldn't make her into a femme fatale even if she opened the gown to her waist. She put on her fleece-lined, ankle-high house shoes and went into the hall.

Before going to the kitchen, she stole a glance into the bedroom. Still sleeping. She watched the slow, steady rise and fall of his chest and felt a return of that earlier, sudden passion she'd felt for him.

She'd never known anything like it. Such a wild rush of desire. No other man had ever incited it. She hadn't thought she was capable of it.

Until Gabe Deveraux.

She thought of how she would greet him when he awoke. "Hi, Gabe"... bright, cheerful, friendly. "Hello, Gabe"... sexy, sultry, alluring. She glanced at her flannel attire. Better stick with bright and cheerful.

She went to see how the soup was doing. After ladling up two bowls to cool, she returned to the bathroom to blow-dry her hair. She was almost finished when she heard a *thump* and a string of groaned curses over the noise of the dryer.

"Oh, no!" She flicked the dryer off and dashed for the bedroom, sure she was going to find Gabe passed out in a heap on the floor, his wound split open from the fall.

She was almost right. He was clinging dizzily to the bed rail. The chair next to the bed was lying on its side.

"What are you doing out of bed?" she demanded, angry in her relief that he hadn't hurt himself. "Are you crazy?"

Putting her arm around his waist and easing his arm over her shoulder, she tried to turn him around and get him back into bed.

He wouldn't budge.

"You've got to get back in bed," she coaxed rather desperately when she realized he was pitting his decreased strength against hers and easily winning.

"Bathroom," he growled, pressing his free hand to his eyes as if fearing they were going to fall out at his next move.

Whitney lowered her voice. "Please get in bed. I'll bring you a . . . um, the milk bottle." She'd been so thoughtless in this regard. Some nurse she was.

"No."

She could tell he regretted the sharp retort by the way he groaned and pressed harder against his head.

"Bathroom," he repeated stubbornly, leaning his weight on her and dragging her in that direction.

"Gabe, please listen to me," she said slowly and carefully. "If you fall, you could do some serious damage."

"Then . . . the sooner we get . . . this done . . . the better."

She could see they weren't going to get anywhere arguing. "All right. Come on. And don't blame me if you fall on your hard head."

He made a sound that could have been a snort of attempted laughter, a curse, or a groan of pain. Step by step, they made it across the room, into the hall and into the bathroom. She paused once she got him inside, unsure what she was supposed to do. Did he need help?

A tide of heat ran up her face at the thought.

"Out!" Gabe ordered. He braced a hand on the wall, the other on the sink, and waited until the world stopped spinning.

"I . . . maybe I'd better . . . stay," she suggested.

"I'm not a baby. I don't need help to go potty." He was sorry for the sarcasm as soon as he said the words. It was just that he hated being weak in front of her. He wanted to hold her, to make love to her; instead, it was all he could do to keep himself upright in front of her. "Go. Now!"

With calculated movements, he slipped one hand to the front opening of his long johns. That got action out of her. She fled, closing the door without a sound.

He wobbled and clutched the towel rack to steady himself while he answered nature's demands. The bathroom was warm and steamy. The shower curtain around the tub was wet. A picture of her in there, her hair like wet, silky ropes around her...

He realized that was what was different about her. For the first time he'd seen her with her hair loose instead of in a braid or tucked up on top of her head. And it was undeniably *red*.

A shower. That was what he needed. It would perk him right up...wash out the cobwebs that seemed to cling to the edges of his mind and his vision.

Clumsily he yanked until he got the T-shirt off over his head. Then he worked at getting the long johns, splint bootie and sock off. Balancing with great effort, he stepped over the edge of the tub, closed the curtain behind him and turned on the water.

Ah, bliss. Warm. Wonderful. Like—what the hell was her name? He'd ask when he returned to the bedroom.

He'd just worked up a shampoo lather—no easy feat when he could only use one hand at a time—when the shower curtain was whisked aside and a great rush of cold air swirled around him.

Gabe opened his eyes in pleased surprise. She was going to join him.

"I can't believe this!" she said.

No maidenly blush on those cheeks now that they were alone, he noted in satisfaction. In fact, her blue eyes ran all over him, as if she couldn't decide what part to devour first.

Hell, he didn't think he was physically all that impressive. However, all modesty aside, he was well endowed and women seemed to appreciate the fact—

"You idiot!"

He blinked. That didn't sound very loverlike.

"What are you trying to do—kill yourself?"

Oh, she was angry. The idea slowly percolated through the haze in his brain. He looked around to see what he'd messed up.

Women hated it when men left messy bathrooms. The woman who'd taken him in when he'd been sixteen had taught him that...and some other things... Well, never mind.

"I'm trying to take a shower," he announced with what he thought was great dignity and maybe a smidgen of indignation tossed in. He wasn't intimidated by a redhead.

She jerked on his arm. "Get the soap rinsed out of your hair. If we can get you back to bed without injury, I'm going to kill you."

With that promise, she pulled a stool over to the tub with her toes, stood on it and forced his head under the stream of water.

He smiled. "Hey, if you wanted to take a shower with me, all you had to do was say so." Wrapping an arm around her waist, he hoisted her into the bathtub with only a tiny wobble.

She shrieked like a banshee.

"Thunderation, Irish, don't you know my head is splitting?" He groaned and put both hands over his ears when she continued to rail at him. Blasted women. A man couldn't tell from one minute to the next what they wanted.

"You are totally insane," she continued, calling him various other names for no reason he could see. He was the one being reasonable. She was the troublemaker.

"Enough," he finally said, frowning ferociously at her. "I'm not going to be yelled at by a redheaded harridan—" What was the rest of that thought? Oh, yes, "Wearing a flannel sack."

Then he noticed how the wet flannel clung to her slender figure, outlining her small, perfectly formed breasts. He reached out to touch her, this tiny piece of paradise who'd fallen into his arms and his bath like a rainbow's treasure.

"You're beautiful," he said, feeling the shape of her hard nipple against his palm. He closed his eyes and leaned against the wall, enjoying this unexpected treat.

"Oh, for heaven's sake," she said. His hands were firmly removed. "Be still. I'll try to get you out of here before you fall on your face. Don't pass out on me," she ordered in drill sergeant tones.

"I won't," he promised, groggily holding on to the curtain rod and soap dish. He experienced a sweet sense of happiness. He couldn't remember the last time he'd felt that.

She muttered a bit more, but her hands were soothingly gentle when she washed the lemon-scented shampoo out of his hair.

"Lift your arm," she ordered.

When he did, she swished a soapy cloth under it, then the other. She washed his face and neck and ears, his arms and torso, legs and feet. The best part was just beginning when she stepped out of the tub and ordered him to hurry and finish before she caught pneumonia standing in a wet gown.

He was disgruntled by her abdication. After all, he was the one who was injured. He finished his bath and pushed the curtain aside. She wore a terry robe and held an oversize towel ready for him. He meekly let her dry him off, a thing no one had done for him since he was a baby.

His mother, what he remembered of her before she'd died, had been too busy with ranch chores to fuss over him. She'd been a quiet woman, not like this harridan—angel, he corrected, feeling tenderly toward her and more than ready for bed.

Gabe opened his eyes and gazed down at her hair, its fiery color tamed somewhat by dampness. She dried off his legs and feet before standing and wrapping the towel around his waist.

"There," she said with evident relief.

He worried briefly about performing with that granddaddy of all headaches beating in his skull. He decided he'd better wait another day. He didn't want to disappoint her....

"I have some soup ready," she told him, leading him to bed.

His sprained ankle was sore, but it wasn't impossible to walk on it. The doctor had indicated the cold was probably what had kept it from being a worse injury. She put the bootie back on him before pushing him prone in the bed and covering him.

"I'm not hungry." Except for the taste and feel of her, but he didn't say that. After all, he had some finesse.

"Here," she said. She handed him an oversize T-shirt, then helped him pull it on. The cloth had been warmed.

His angel was going to unman him if she kept this up. Her tenderness, the way she looked at him, letting him see the hunger in her for him, even her angry concern, did something strange to his insides. She touched places that he hadn't even known existed. That could be bad for a man in his position.

She brought food to the room on a tray. Sitting on the bed, she spooned a thick, stick-to-the-ribs soup into him. It was delicious.

"Thanks, Irish," he remembered to say when it was gone. She gave him a drink of water and two pills.

"For what?"

"For supper. The soup was good. Did you make it?"

"Yes. What did you call me?"

He tried to think. His brain was going muzzy again. "Irish," he finally said.

"Why?" She seemed vitally interested in his reply.

"Your eyes are like the sea off the coast there, so deep a blue, a man could fall in and sink forever." He looked into those drowning depths. He could feel himself going once...going twice...

If he went down the third time, he'd never get out. He remembered he had a job to do, then he was getting the hell away from the ranch and all its hateful memories, away from the small town and its small-minded people.

He pulled his gaze away with an effort and glanced around the homey room. She was building her nest. Next thing, she'd be looking for a mate to share it with her. He wasn't a candidate for the domestic scene.

"I...my name is Whitney. Whitney Thompson."

"Thompson. Sounds familiar."

"My grandparents lived here, then my grandmother stayed on after Grandfather died."

He remembered them vaguely. He'd known his neighbors to speak to, but he'd never had an occasion to socialize with them. He and his father had stuck close to the ranch.

He was too tired to think any longer. Instead he gave himself entirely into her hands and let her tuck him in, covering him to his chin with the sweet-smelling sheet and blankets.

Slipping into darkness that was warm and secure, different from last night—no, the night before—when the dark had boded death, he relaxed completely. His dreams took over.

In them, he ran across a green meadow. He held a woman's hand in his. When he looked at her, her hair was like flames dancing all around her laughing face.

A man would risk anything to possess such a dream.

Chapter Four

Whitney changed out of her robe into a comfortable sweat suit, black with hot-pink stripes down the sides, one of her Christmas presents from her father and stepmother. She put on socks, then her warm booties. After returning to the bedroom, she added a log to the fire. Settling in the recliner, she observed her patient.

Gabe Deveraux was a man of unusual strength and powers of recovery. After the episode in the shower, she'd decided to sleep in the chair. It was better not to tempt fate.

Fate? It was her own rebellious instincts she had to quell. Some stubborn part of her insisted that he belonged to her.

Finders keepers didn't apply to people, she sternly told that foolish part. He was a drifter, a man who'd roamed the world on his own for years. He was probably as reliable as others of his sex, and she could testify to the fact that men weren't to be depended on, going by her recent experiences with the handyman and the furnace repairman.

The bedsprings creaked as he shifted restlessly. He'd thrown the blankets off. She got up and covered him.

His hand snaked out and caught her hair, causing her to gasp. His reflexes were honed to a knife edge. Even in sleep, he kept up a sharp vigilance on all that was around him. Her heart went out to a man who'd lived a life that dangerous.

She started to ease her hair out of his grip.

"Talk to me." He sounded hoarse.

"You need to sleep." She touched his forehead. Hot. Glancing at the clock, she saw it was time for his pills.

"Can't. Too restless." He opened his eyes. His pupils were the same size, and his eyes seemed to focus okay. His concussion was rapidly improving.

When he moved over, she sat on the side of the bed. After giving him two antibiotic capsules and a drink of water, she tried to think of something to say.

"What are you doing here?" he asked.

That question brought a smile to her lips. She looked at him, then paused. For a strange second, reality faded, and she felt as if she were being drawn into the dark fire of his soul. He stared at her as if he felt it, too. Then he blinked and looked away.

Shaken, she started talking at random. "I always loved this place. When I'd visit in the summer, my grandparents would take me fishing and hiking. We'd climb the hill over the creek and have a picnic. I hated September. That's when I had to leave. I vowed to come back and live here when I grew up."

She paused, remembering the nights she'd cried after she went to bed, longing to return here.

"This was my true home," she said softly. "My heart's home." She smiled as she remembered the young girl she'd been. Her dreams hadn't changed at all when she'd grown up.

But she'd learned to be more practical, she reminded herself, rousing from her nostalgia.

"You're here to live...to stay?" His frown was daunting.

"Yes."

"Alone?"

"Not exactly. I'm going to convert the house into a bed-and-breakfast inn."

"I see." He plainly didn't like the idea.

She became defensive. "With the increased tourist trade in Ashland for the Shakespeare festival in the summer, in addition to the popularity of the resort north of here, the business should do very well."

Her banker thought so, too, but she didn't bother to add this tidbit of information. It was none of Gabe Deveraux's business. He'd certainly done nothing with his inheritance.

He pushed himself upright against the pillows. She waited for a scoffing remark. Instead he lifted a lock of her hair, which she hadn't bothered to rebraid after the scene in the shower. He stroked the wildly curling end across his palm again and again, his face pensive.

"What are your dreams?" she dared to ask.

He met her gaze head-on. "I gave up on dreams a long time ago," he said coolly.

"When you were sixteen and left home?"

His fist closed on the curl. The bleakness in his eyes nearly caused her to cry out. She'd seen that anguish once before in him.

"What do you know about that?" he demanded. His change of mood was startling.

"My grandmother told me about it after...after your father...When you came home...the time I saw you at the cemetery."

Like a door closing, all emotion left him. But not before she glimpsed the anguish that had called out to her during the encounter so many years ago, right before his grim expression had frightened her into running away. Then he'd been ready to lash out at anyone who came too close; now he simply shut himself off.

She touched the thin line of his lips. She was older, too. She wouldn't run from him the way she had that hot summer day so long ago. "You looked so sad," she murmured.

He took her hand in his. Instead of thrusting her away, though, he pressed it against his chest. Beneath the T-shirt she'd given him, she felt the increasing beat of his heart.

"You could make a man forget all he'd ever learned of life, Irish." He gave a snort of laughter, cynical and self-directed. "Your eyes invite a man into your soul."

Slowly she shook her head, her eyes locked with his. She was the one drawn inside. "Only you," she whispered, her throat so tight it hurt to speak.

The moment lengthened into an eternity. She was captivated, pulled willingly into the vast darkness of his spirit. She recognized the anguish he so carefully hid, the goodness he locked away, the tenderness he wouldn't admit to. She wanted to stay there forever, locked inside him—

"Why?" he demanded in a rough tone. "You don't know me."

"Oh, yes," she said. "I know you." She realized it was true. He belonged here just as she did. He'd returned just as she had. Two pilgrims, looking for home.

"Did you come back to claim your inheritance?" she asked. She felt so tender toward him, it caused an ache in her breast.

He shook his head, then released her hand and the lock of hair. "Give me a couple more painkillers. Maybe you'll feel safe enough to come to bed then, and we can both get some sleep."

He slumped into the pillows. The fatigue had caught up with him, she saw. She gave him the pills, then touched his forehead again as he drifted into sleep. He looked at her once more, a deep, probing search for something that only he knew. He almost smiled, then he closed his eyes.

She sat by him for a long time, watching him. His dreams seemed calmer than during his earlier sleep.

Finders keepers? she questioned.

Yes. They had found each other, lost souls who were destined to meet. They belonged here, both of them. On this surety, she returned to the chair to tend the fire during the rest of the stormy night.

"Out of town? Your sister's place? In California?"

Whitney repeated fragments of sentences as Mr. Peters explained why he couldn't get out there for the foreseeable future. The news was a low blow, and she was still in shock.

"I dropped by Friday to tell you," he said righteously.

She remembered the mysterious tracks in the snow. "Why didn't you come in? I left the door open."

"You shouldn't go off without locking up. Strange doings at the place next door," he warned in ominous tones, changing the topic from his sins to hers.

"Huh," she scoffed, unmoved by his fake concern.

"I'll see you in the spring," he said, and hung up.

She put the old-fashioned black phone on the hook and stared out the windows across the living room. Fresh snow was falling. It was breaking all previous records in amounts and frequency.

Fighting anger and frustration, she buoyed up her spirits with the decision to get on with the work. She could do it. All she needed was a book or two to give her some helpful hints.

Peering in the alcove under the wide stairs, she studied the layout of the hallway. By tearing out the closet next to the alcove, the area would do for reception and check-out, unobtrusive but handy to the front door.

Walking down the hall, she glanced into her room to check on the patient. He was sitting in the recliner in front of the fire, which was blazing over the fresh logs he'd obviously added.

"What are you doing?" she demanded, charging into the room and stopping by the chair.

"Warming my feet."

"Lie down. I'll heat some towels and—"

"I'm fine."

She pointed a finger at the bed. "Get in that bed. Now! The doctor said you were to stay put for three days—"

"I'll decide where I stay and how long."

The words were softly spoken, but there was nothing soft in the willpower that backed them. Startled by the hardness of his gaze, she hesitated, not sure what to do.

To her utter consternation, tears filled her eyes. "Fine. I'll make some tea," she said in a choked voice.

"Irish—"

She turned from the doorway and rushed into the kitchen, on the brink of falling apart. She stopped by the pantry and leaned her forehead against the cool panes of glass, searching for composure, fighting despair.

Mr. Peters's defection was a setback, not a disaster, she reminded herself sternly. She'd find someone else to help.

As for Gabe Deveraux, he could go to the devil. She hadn't asked for his exalted presence in her home, eating her food and occupying her bed, taking time away from her important tasks. The next time she got the urge to play Florence Nightingale, she would adopt a mangy dog.

She rubbed her neck. The blizzard had arrived in a fury of blowing wind and driven snow during the night, chilling the house. She'd hardly slept just to keep the fire going... so *he* wouldn't get cold and catch pneumonia.

Pressing a hand over her burning eyes, she realized she was tired. That was why her spirits were so low this morning.

Gabe had been restless during the night, moving his head from side to side and muttering occasionally as his dreams became violent. He'd thrown the covers off more than once.

A hand touched her shoulder, making her jump.

"I'm sorry," he said, moving back a step and dropping his hold on her. He seemed angry that he found it necessary to apologize.

She lifted her chin and gave him a cool appraisal. "You were entirely within your rights. After all, I'm not your keeper."

He gazed deeply into her eyes, pinning her to the spot. For a moment he seemed to be inviting her into those depths. Fighting the sensation, she swallowed the knot of tension that had lodged in her throat and looked away.

"I'll help you with the work," he said, his voice gentler.

He'd obviously heard the telephone conversation and deduced that Mr. Peters had reneged on his promise. She looked at Gabe's splinted foot. Some help he would be. She bit back the sarcastic retort.

His impatient sigh brought her gaze to his face. "I'll be good as new when my ankle heals. The swelling is almost gone. I, uh, could use a job."

Her conscience chided her for the uncharitable thoughts. She realized he must need money. His ranch hadn't been worked in years, so he had no income there, and taxes still had to be paid, come hell or high water.

She thought of him working on the house with her. It brought a yearning to her heart so acute she had to put a hand to her chest to still the frantic beat.

"I'm good with my hands," he added sardonically. His glance slid down her jeans-clad figure. "Although I may have trouble keeping them to myself." This last was muttered more to himself than to her.

The betraying heat climbed into her face. She stared at him, not sure how to respond. No one had ever spoken to her with a lover's inflection in his tone, as if she were so incredibly desirable he might not be able to control himself around her.

It gave her a heady feeling...if she let herself believe such blarney. She wouldn't be so foolish, as she'd been last night, imagining they belonged together.

She considered all the reasons she shouldn't hire him. "The job pays ten dollars an hour," she said. She must be crazy.

"I'll take it."

His acceptance came so fast, she almost didn't believe it. She recalled he had a room at the resort. That had to be terribly expensive, and there weren't any rooming houses in town. "It includes room and board."

There was a short pause—one of those described in books as pregnant. She felt the full portent of the word while she waited for his response.

"Fine," he said, a hooded expression falling over his eyes.

A coldness came over her. She felt as if he'd just closed a door in her face, but she'd witnessed relief in his eyes before he'd blanked out all expression. He must be desperate, but was too proud to say so.

Her heart ached for him. She knew about pride. She wanted her place to be the best B&B in the state.

"Shall I arrange to get your things from the lodge?" She heard the tenderness in her voice and wondered if he did, too.

"I'm not in the lodge. I'm staying with friends." He stopped, then said, "I'll call and have them send my things over."

There was a stiffness in his manner. He'd definitely put a barrier between them. She nodded and moved away. At the stove, she turned on the gas under a burner and set a pot of water to boil for tea.

"There's coffee cake. Would you like some with your tea?"

When there was no answer, she glanced around. He was gone as quietly as he'd arrived.

On an impulse, she ran to the door and saw him walking toward the chair in front of the fireplace in the bedroom. In the heavy sock and the bootie, he made no sound on the oak flooring. It was almost eerie to see a man his size move so silently.

Questions about his past ran endlessly through her mind while she prepared the midmorning snack. She kept them to herself.

She didn't hear him make the call, but an hour later a utility vehicle from the ski resort arrived, pushing through the thick snow in the lane. A young man with the resort logo on his pocket delivered a suitcase and a nylon duffel bag to the door.

She led the way to the bedroom.

The young man said he had a message for Gabe from Rafe Barrett. Then he waited for her to leave.

Excusing herself, she retreated into the hall. Standing by the telephone alcove, she wondered when Gabe had called the resort. And why the resort owner—she'd recognized the name—would have a private message for him.

An uneasy premonition settled on her. Gabe Deveraux was a mystery. She knew very little about him. Perhaps she was foolish to give him a job and free access to her home.

This place was her dream. A wrong decision could ruin it. She wrapped her arms across her chest as another dream imposed itself on her old ones—one in which she shared her life with a special man, a man with eyes that seemed to look upon ancient vistas, a man whose heart was filled with dreams as dear as hers.

While the storm piled snow to record heights, she demolished the wall separating a small front parlor from the antechamber. That opened the living area into a spacious room of pleasing proportions that went with the high ceilings. While she worked, she was acutely aware of her guest prowling the house.

Like a black mountain cat, he moved with lithe grace and in total silence. Several times that morning, she'd found him close by, leaning against the wall, watching her work.

Once in a while she'd catch a glimpse of something in his eyes that would cause her breath to tangle in her throat. Like a dark intruder, he invaded her every thought, waking and sleeping.

That afternoon, done with the living room, she turned to the alcove. The closet was next to go. It was enclosed with wooden panels, a snap to remove. She carried the panels to the basement and cleaned up the dust.

At five, she headed for the shower.

She stopped when she heard a noise coming from the basement. Gabe must be wandering around down there. She wished he would be careful. He could trip and hurt himself again.

In her mind's eye, she saw him lying in the snow, struck over the head and left for dead by some unknown villain. She hadn't entirely accepted his owl-and-falling-timber story.

After all, he'd been in the vicinity for at least a week. He surely had had plenty of time to explore the old house by the light of day rather than the light of the moon. She remembered Mrs. Tall's warning about lights over at the ranch. Maybe she'd better be a bit more cautious.

Retrieving the crowbar she'd used on the wall, she tiptoed to the basement door. With her heart thumping, she listened but heard nothing else. Slowly, carefully, she reached over to turn the knob. The door swung open. She stared into midnight-dark eyes.

"What's happening?" Gabe asked, coming into the hall and closing the door behind him. He wiped his hands on an oily rag.

Feeling ridiculous, she lowered the crowbar and stared at him. "What do you think you're doing?" she demanded, her worry turning to anger at him for scaring her.

"Turning on the furnace."

"It's broken. It needs a new valve."

He shook his head. "The controls needed a minor adjustment. Otherwise, it works fine. There was a service tag attached to the gas line. The system was cleaned and repaired eight years ago. I'd say it hasn't been used since."

"The repairman said it needed major work," she argued inanely. "He's supposed to fix it next week."

"Cancel the appointment," Gabe advised. A feral smile appeared at the corners of his mouth, and he looked dangerous once more. "Or let him show up, and I'll discuss the matter with him."

Whitney felt the full force of Gabe's masculine power. She'd never had anyone offer to take on her problems before. It gave her a strange sensation, on top of feeling naive and gullible. She'd believed the repairman.

"Thanks, but I'll cancel."

"That's probably best." He nodded toward the basement stairs. "There's furniture down there. Also in the attic."

He'd taken a thorough look at the house from top to bottom. She wondered what he was looking for. Maybe he was "casing the joint" for valuables he planned to steal later. Instinctively she knew that wasn't true. "It's mostly junk. The good stuff disappeared long ago."

"Into relatives' homes, no doubt."

She was surprised at his insight. "It wasn't clear in the will if the furniture went with the house. The probate court let the immediate family choose their favorite pieces."

"But the house was willed to you?"

"Yes." She wondered what he was getting at.

"That *junk* you spoke of is solid wood—oak, maple, ash, some walnut pieces. If it were repaired and refinished, it would be as good as new."

Gabe watched a pleased smile bloom on her face. Again, it curled up inside him, giving him a sense of peace and contentment. He frowned. He couldn't afford feelings of any kind.

He had a job to do—find the thieves using the ranch and clear his name, then he'd sell the place and be free of its unhappy memories forever. Until then, he'd keep his distance from this redheaded siren who stirred impossible dreams in him.

To do that, he reasoned, he needed to stay occupied. While exploring the old house to work off excess energy, he'd reviewed his plan. Now that his head didn't hurt quite so much and his leg could take his weight, he'd start to repay his debt to her by helping with the renovation project.

The work would give him an excuse to keep an eye on his ranch without arousing suspicion. Like Whitney, the townspeople would think he needed the money.

He looked at the plan from all angles. Yeah, it would work. He glanced at his employer. If he could keep his hands to himself... Nest building wasn't in his future. When he cleared out the polecats using his ranch for a storage depot, he'd sell the place and be off on the next flight out.

"When do you plan to open for business?" he asked.

"As soon as possible." She frowned, then wrinkled her nose as if laughing at herself. "Easter. I hope."

Her eyes sparkled. She was the most trusting person he'd ever met. Or the most foolhardy. She'd taken him, a total stranger, into her home without a single thought that she might be in danger.

He'd have to teach her not to be so trusting. Some man would come along and take advantage of that innocence.

"What about your ranch?" she asked. "You'll need to repair the fences if you're going to run cattle. Oh! Mrs. Tall said there'd been lights at your place and warned me..."

Her voice trailed off, and Gabe watched confusion flicker into her eyes. He waited for the familiar wariness to appear.

The townspeople had been quick to be suspicious of him years ago when theft was discovered and some of the goods were found hidden on the ranch. Even his own father hadn't believed him, but had taken a belt to him for lying when he'd insisted he knew nothing about the stuff. He'd never forgiven the old man for that last injustice. He'd taken the walloping, then left home as soon as his father went to bed that night.

Now, to his astonishment, his beautiful rescuer didn't look at him with any suspicion at all. Instead she questioned him, her face earnest as she worried over him and his ranch.

"Is someone using your ranch for illegal purposes? Did you catch them, and then did they hit you to shut you up? We should call the sheriff at once—"

"No," he cut in. "It was as I said, an accident."

She mulled this over. "I don't believe you."

"You think the roof didn't cave in on me? You should see my inheritance." He gave her a mocking smile. "Better watch that imagination, Irish. Life isn't a John Wayne movie." And he sure as hell wasn't going to be the hero who gets the lovely lady in the end.

He watched the red creep into her face. Her fair skin reflected her every emotion. He wondered how she would look when she was replete with lovemaking.

That wasn't going to happen, he reminded himself savagely.

"You'd better watch out for yourself," she informed him. "Ranchers hereabouts have been known to shoot first and ask questions later, especially when strangers lurk around in the woods for no good reason."

The discussion was getting heated. He changed the subject. "I found a bed in one of the rooms upstairs. I'll move in there and let you have your quarters again."

A flicker of disappointment hit her face and was quickly gone. It was all he could do not to take her into his arms. She'd wrap him in the silky bonds of her allure if he didn't watch himself, and he'd forget why he was there...and why he had to leave.

"I remember it. The slats are broken, aren't they?"

"I found some boards in the basement that fit. I'll fix it."

She nodded, her candid gaze studying him as if she could see inside and knew every lie that he'd ever told. He sighed. She was a complication he could live without.

Whitney made no comment while Gabe repaired the bed. When he carried his luggage upstairs, she followed with sheets, blankets and a pillow from her bed.

"You found a feather mattress," she said in surprise when she bent to smooth the sheet on.

"Yeah. There's a couple more in the attic."

His mood was introspective. Respecting his privacy, she said nothing further, but finished the bed and left the room. Going to the kitchen, she checked the lasagna she'd put in to bake. Almost done. She sliced French bread, buttered it and stuck it in the oven to heat while she made a salad.

When the meal was ready, she looked through her boxes until she found place mats and napkins. These she put on the small table in her quarters. She went to the kitchen and loaded a tray.

When she returned to the bed-sitting-room, Gabe was there. He stood at the window, one hand on the frame, while he gazed toward the west where his ranch was. Night had turned the sky black. The snow fell in endless silence.

Flames danced cheerily in the hearth, she noted, pleased that he'd built a fire. He shifted and sighed.

The rogue was restless.

Ignoring the clamor in her heart, she set the dishes on the table and hurried to the kitchen for the wine and glasses. She'd decided to make it a festive occasion to lighten the mood, which had been decidedly broody all day.

"Dinner," she announced gaily upon her return.

He turned and looked at her, his gaze dark and angry. It caused her smile to falter for a second. She poured wine into her glass. "Would you like a glass of wine?" she asked politely. "It's red and aged at least a month."

A smile flickered at the corners of his mouth and was gone. When he nodded, she filled his glass. He came to the table.

"Allow me," he said, and held her chair.

When he sat down, his foot touched hers. She moved hers self-consciously, but not before she'd felt a tingle at the contact.

"The roads will be closed until this storm lets up," he said.

She sensed his wish to escape. "Yes." She picked up her fork. They started on the salad and bread. Only the crackle of the fire broke the tense silence.

He would help her for a few days, then he would be gone. She knew it. She removed the salad plates and brought in the main course. She served herself, then let him do the same.

"This is delicious," he commented.

"Thank you." She sipped the wine and gazed into the fire. Her mood darkened to match his. She forced herself to be social. "Are you going to restock your ranch?" she asked.

An idea came to her. They could combine their holdings. With a working ranch plus the B&B, it would be a sort of dude ranch operation, but with cross-country skiing, fishing and hiking, as well as riding and helping with the cattle.

"No. I'm going to sell it in the spring."

"You're going to sell your home?" She was shocked.

His expression hardened, closing her out. "It's hardly a home," he remarked. "The roof is falling in and the windows let in more air than they keep out."

"But someday you might want to return to it." At his slicing glance, she stopped the advice. "I wish I could buy it," she said impulsively. "Maybe I could lease the land from you—"

"No, I want to sell."

The quickness of his refusal hurt. She forced a nonchalant shrug. "I haven't the financial resources..."

"You've thought of something. What is it?" he demanded.

"Well, it crossed my mind to ask my mother and stepfather if they'd like to go in with me, but that's a bad idea. They'd feel they have the right to interfere." She stopped before she exposed too much.

"The way they have in the past?" He seemed to know of her life without her having to explain. It was disconcerting.

"They mean well," she said softly to defuse his temper. "It's just that Mom has always thought she knew what was best for me."

"But you don't agree?"

Whitney shook her head. The braid slipped forward across her shoulder. She pushed it behind her back, aware that his gaze followed her every move. It made her nervous and breathless, the way he looked at her.

He was edgy tonight. If the weather hadn't been so terrible, he'd have been out prowling, looking for... what?

"What were you doing at your ranch last week?" she ventured. All he could do was snap her head off for asking, she decided with fatalistic humor. "I saw you several times in the woods."

"Yeah, I didn't know anyone was living here until I saw your light in the window and the smoke from the chimney."

"You weren't pleased." She deduced this from his tone.

He grinned, and her heart swooned. "I'd planned to use your place as a temporary shelter while I checked the ranch out."

She gasped. "You were going to break in?"

The sardonic smile disappeared. "I've done worse things."

It was a warning, and it burned all the way down inside her. "Only for good reasons," she said through a tight throat.

She wouldn't believe evil of him. She'd looked into his soul and seen anguish and loneliness, but not evil... never that!

For a second he looked so strange, as if emotions too powerful to be contained pushed against his skin. He laid his fork down and glared at her.

"My God," he muttered, "but you could destroy a man."

Whitney bit into her lower lip and remained silent while he pressed a hand to his eyes as if he had a headache. She didn't understand. She didn't want to destroy anyone. She wanted...

She stared into the fire, awash with feelings too long denied while she'd worked for her dream. She'd done it gladly, but now she realized there was more to living. This man had forced her to acknowledge the inner person she'd only vaguely been aware of. And that inner person wanted to share life.

When she sighed shakily, he lowered his hand and looked at her. For a long minute she couldn't look away.

"Guard yourself," he said hoarsely. "Don't ever depend on anyone. They'll only let you down."

Anger stirred on his behalf. Someone he'd trusted had let him down. It was a wound that had never healed.

Or was he talking about her and him? Was he warning her not to fall in love with him because she'd get hurt? She lifted her chin. "I can take care of myself," she said. She stood and gathered the dishes and carried them to the kitchen.

Chapter Five

Whitney had expected Gabe to retire to his room, but he was at the window when she returned, gazing out as if his soul longed to be free. She didn't understand him at all, but something about him tugged at her heart strings. She wanted to take him into her arms and comfort him for all the wrongs life had dealt him.

Foolish, she reminded herself. Compassion was okay in its place, but she mustn't allow it to get out of hand.

"How about a game of poker?" she asked brightly.

He swung around, a skeptical smile on his face. "Poker?"

"Sure. I play a mean game," she warned. She dug around in a box and came up with the cards. At the table, she expertly shuffled them and set the deck out for him to cut.

He took his chair and cut the cards.

"Five card draw," she said. "Queen of hearts wild."

She wished the words back when he scowled at her, his glance as cutting as volcanic glass. She dealt, then picked up her cards. The queen of hearts was her last card. She put it with a pair of tens for three of a kind.

"What are we going to bet?" he asked. "Got any matches?"

"Oh, I forgot." She searched through the boxes stacked in a corner of the room. "Toothpicks okay?"

He grunted assent. They each put one toothpick in for the ante; then he added one. She did the same.

"One," Gabe said, laying one card face down on the table.

After dealing him one card, she discarded and dealt two for herself. She stared at the cards, her mind on her opponent.

He was a rogue with a rogue's heart—wild and untamed. He would never let himself need anyone. He wouldn't let anyone get that close. He wasn't *hers*. She couldn't clip his wings and make him stay if he didn't want it, too.

The pressure of tears built behind her eyes, a thing that didn't often happen to her. She wasn't given to weeping. But something about this man saddened her. It was as if she'd seen all the broken dreams in his heart when she'd looked into his eyes that first time at the cemetery.

She sighed and put the thought behind her. She could be all wrong about him. Perhaps he was a cold, hard man who was incapable of caring for anyone. Anyway, she'd better concentrate on the cards. She'd suggested the game to distract him from whatever was making him so restless.

She raised the pot by one toothpick. He called her. She won easily over his busted straight. They settled into play, observing each other's strategy without speaking. The hours ticked by.

"Where'd you learn to play?" he asked at one point. She wasn't playing badly, but she was slowly losing, her cards a mess after that first successful hand.

"The guys at college. I was practically the only female with a world affairs major. We used to hold all-night poker marathons after midterms and finals."

"I see." He looked disapproving.

"I was just one of the gang," she quickly added. She'd liked the guys, but none of them had been special.

His gaze slid over her. "They must have been blind," he muttered, a note of disbelief in his words.

With great difficulty, she quelled the ridiculous pride that filled her. If he kept saying things like that, she might begin to believe him. And that would be foolish.

Her mother had wanted her to be a social success and marry some prince, either of a country or an industry. Instead, Whitney had been a tomboy and a bookworm. She knew her limitations, but now she admitted she wished she were more of a femme fatale. Perhaps then she'd know how to hold this rogue....

At ten o'clock, then eleven, she tried to quit, but he insisted on giving her a chance to recoup her losses. At twelve, she bet her last toothpick and lost.

"Is this luck, or are you cheating?" she demanded.

"Them's fightin' words," he warned.

"Sorry." She yawned. "I'm cleaned out. Game's over," she announced, actually relieved to have it end.

"One more hand."

"I'll have to find more toothpicks."

"Wager something else."

"What?" She gave him a disgruntled glare.

"A kiss."

She blinked in the sudden quiet. His gaze challenged her, visibly calling her a coward when she hesitated. He seemed in a reckless mood. She glanced at the clock. Midnight. The witching hour. A thrill raced along her nerves.

"All right." She accepted the dare. She pushed her hair behind her shoulder and stared at the cards as he dealt them one by one onto the table.

"Queen of hearts wild." He pushed his stack of toothpicks into the center.

"All or nothing?" she questioned. "A wise player saves something for another day."

"Play or fold."

She took a breath and picked up her cards. The last one was the queen of hearts. She hadn't seen that lady since the first hand they'd played. Whitney knew she was going to win.

Disappointment swept over her. For a fraction of a heartbeat, she thought of pretending she didn't see the four card straight that the queen would fill out into a strong hand. But she couldn't cheat, not even to lose.

She kept the cards she'd been dealt. He drew one. He smiled, just the slightest upturn of the corners of his mouth, as if very pleased with his hand.

"Two pairs," he said, laying the cards on the table. His eyes flicked to her.

"A straight." She put it down. She'd been losing all night, why win now?

His smile changed, becoming rueful. "Hell."

She pulled the toothpicks toward her side of the table with an angry motion. When she glanced at him, his expression had changed again. Now he looked thoughtful.

"You can have the kiss," he said.

Her heart thundered. "I won." She sounded breathless.

"But you want the kiss."

"I..." But she couldn't force the lie past her lips. The blood pounded into her face, giving her away.

He rose and stepped to the side of her chair. His hand took hers, lifting her to her feet by the force of his will. When they stood toe-to-toe, he dipped his head slightly. He paused, and she thought she would die from disappointment. Then he licked his lips and settled them softly on her mouth.

The sensation was stunning. She couldn't stop the tremor that shook through her like an earthquake.

He lifted his head and studied her. "You make me wild when you do that," he whispered.

"What?"

"Tremble. As if you can't wait..."

He made a sound low in his throat and pulled her close. He wrapped his hand around her braid so she couldn't move her head from his grasp. She didn't want to move.

His lips seared hers—hot and urgent. She responded as best she could. Wild passion wasn't something she was used to. She'd kissed, yes. She'd done some exploring of the passionate side of the male-female relationship, but not completely and not like this.

The kiss deepened. He stroked across her lips with his tongue, seeking entry. She opened her mouth to his.

The wildness of the storm outside became part of the tempest within. A wind, driven by desire, rushed through her. She clung to him, shaking with the force of it.

His hands roamed her back, communicating the restless energy locked within him. She sensed his need for more. She wanted more, too, but she wasn't sure how to tell him.

She wrapped her arms around his shoulders and answered the moist heat of his mouth on hers. Flames burned deep inside, turning caution to cinders. Her legs were trembling so, she could hardly stand. He touched her breast, and she stiffened.

He released her at once. She cried out softly, not wanting the contact to end.

"No, don't," he said when she would have stepped close again.

She stopped, confusion replacing passion. She turned away, embarrassed by her runaway emotions.

His arms closed around her waist. He pressed his face against her hair, his chest against her back. "Don't you understand? I can't just kiss you and let it go at that."

"That's what you just did," she remarked in her usual, candid style. The fire blurred before her eyes. She felt foolish, not sure what he wanted or expected.

He sighed. "In another minute, I'd have taken you to that bed over there and not let you go until morning."

She tried to protest, but couldn't.

"You couldn't have stopped me," he said. "I wouldn't have let you. You don't know the extent of your own passion."

"I—I do," she lied. She was fast getting some ideas about that. And about his desire. She pressed against him.

He caught his breath. His arms tightened at her waist. "You little hellion," he muttered, his breath tickling her ear. "I'm the one giving lessons around here."

"Lessons?" She twisted around to face him.

"Lessons," he repeated, his face stony. "You're too gullible. You open your home and your—" his dark gaze swept down her body "—heart to strangers, trusting them to be as honest as you are. Life doesn't work that way."

Humiliation poured over her. She must be totally transparent. Thrusting her chin into the air, she looked him in the eye. "You wanted me, too."

"I still do," he said with a rueful grimace. "If we'd made love..." He shook his head, as if words failed him.

"What?" she demanded, entranced, wanting to hear what would have happened.

He touched her lips with fingers that trembled slightly. "It would have been mind-blowing. Powerful beyond anything you ever imagined."

She made a little choked sound as she thought of what they'd given up. "Why did you stop?" she whispered.

"Because a wise person doesn't get that close to anyone." He spoke with great finality and dropped his hand.

"Why?" she cried. "Why, if it's so wonderful?"

He smiled, but it was resigned and perhaps a bit regretful. "It's best that way. You have your dreams, and I have . . . mine."

But she knew that wasn't what he'd been about to say. He was a man without dreams.

He walked away from her. At the hearth, he added logs to the fire to keep her room warmer than the furnace could manage during the night. She thought of his chilly room upstairs.

"If you stayed here, we could share warmth," she said. "We did that first night. I slept with you."

"I know." He glanced over his shoulder at her, the fire behind him, backlighting him so that he looked like part of a painting, too beautiful to be real. "When you came to bed . . . When you trusted me . . ." He shook his head.

"I do trust you."

"For now." He stood. "But what about when things get tough?"

On that enigmatic question, he headed for the door. She listened to his steps on the stairs, barely audible above the whine of the wind over the house. A shiver went over her, of cold, not passion. There was a difference, she'd discovered.

"It's nice to have the house warm when I get up," Whitney commented at breakfast. "Thanks for checking out the furnace."

Gabe sat at the kitchen planning area, eating the hot oatmeal she'd prepared that morning. "That's what a handyman is for." He appeared rather glum.

It had been hard to face him after the aborted kiss...one that he'd ended, not her. Taking a deep breath, she forced herself to ignore the undercurrents between them and act as if nothing had happened. However, it was hard not to stare at his mouth and remember the feel of his lips on hers.

Her pulse increased its tempo. She'd always been a pal to her fellow students and workers. It was odd to think of herself as a woman who quite possibly could seduce a man.

"The sun is shining," she said, her spirits lifting. "It's nice to see it after so many days of clouds and snow, isn't it?"

She glanced toward the windows. The whiteness of the snow was blinding in the bright sunlight.

"I'll have to call the snowplow company and have the lane cleared as soon as they can get to it." She thought of being snowed in for days with a special person.

"It's being taken care of."

She looked at him blankly.

His glance flicked to her, lingered a split second on her lips, then moved on. "Rafe Barrett said he'd tell his crew to run the plow along your road when they finish at the resort."

As if to prove his words, they heard the low growl of a diesel engine approaching the house from the lane.

"Why would he do that?"

Gabe shrugged. "A good deed from one neighbor to another."

But the resort owner didn't know her from Adam. He was Gabe's friend, that much was obvious. It didn't tie in with her view of Gabe as a drifter and loner. An uneasiness ruffled her heart. There were so many things about him that she didn't understand.

"What are the plans for the day?" he asked.

Whitney focused on the present. "I was going to see if I could find some curtains for the bedroom windows." Now that he was there, she felt self-conscious about someone seeing in.

"There's a bunch of stuff like that in the attic." He gave her a curious glance. "Haven't you explored it yet?"

"No. I only got here a couple of days after Christmas." She wrinkled her nose. "Then I was too busy trying to arrange credit and find someone to help me with the work to check into everything. Cleaning out the attic and basement are pretty far down on my priority list."

"You should go through them."

"I will." She ate her oatmeal standing at the counter. "I think you're going to be a real boon to my business. You're the only one who saw any possibilities in the old furniture."

He shrugged. "Cleaning and repairing it will be a big job. Don't be grateful until it's done."

His warning didn't daunt her. It sounded as if he were planning to do the furniture. That could take a long time.

A smile gave an insistent tug on her mouth. She felt gloriously happy. Foolish, but no words of warning could change what she felt. Finished with her oatmeal, pencil in hand, she worked up a new list of chores.

"What do you want done first today?" he asked.

"You're not well enough—"

His glare cut her off.

"Well," she hedged, trying to think of something he could do that wouldn't be too tiring.

"I'll hang the curtains if you find any you like," he decided. "In the meantime, I'll remove the wall studs where you took the plaster and paneling off."

She frowned, knowing he'd be up on his injured foot. Men. They couldn't admit to a weakness. Maybe she should hit him on the other side of his head to see if she could knock some sense back into him. Giving up on the idea, she said, "I need to wash clothes this morning. If you'll give me your things, I'll do them, too."

He looked startled at this suggestion. "I can take care of my own things."

"You probably don't have a full load. Neither do I. It'll save water and soap and energy to do them all at once," she said briskly. She laid her list aside and began washing up the few dishes they'd used. She smiled at him over her shoulder.

He frowned at her, then looked away. "I'll handle it."

She paused, irritated at his secretive nature. Didn't he think she'd ever seen men's personal clothing? "Don't be silly. I used to share chores with the student who lived in the studio apartment next to mine when I was in school. We took turns doing the laundry."

He gave her a narrow-eyed scrutiny. "You did a man's clothes and he wasn't your lover?"

"Yes." She dried her hands, exasperated at his disbelieving tone. "Men and women can be friends without falling into bed."

"Huh," he snorted.

He seemed to think sharing a washing machine was an act of intimacy. It was hardly the same as sharing a bed, but it gave her a strange feeling to know he found her so alluring that he assumed other men did, too.

Without another word, he limped from the room. In a few minutes he returned, his eyes wary as he laid a small bundle of clothes on the floor. She made no comment.

In the laundry room off the kitchen, she sorted the clothes and started the first load. He was right. Their mixed laundry did seem rather intimate.

Whitney recalled her mother's many lectures on schooling her sharp tongue. She'd always rebelled at the idea that a woman was supposed to bend over backward to please a man, but now, well, she sort of liked fussing over Gabe. She suspected he'd had very little of that in his life.

Humming, she started down the list of chores.

Late in the morning, when the sun had warmed the house, she climbed the steps to the gabled attic.

It was divided into three rooms—a big one in the middle, where the stairs were, and two smaller ones on each side of it. Each room was piled to the ceiling with furniture, boxes and steamer trunks.

She began a methodical search for the curtains Gabe had mentioned. She found keepsakes from her grandmother's life—dance cards and pressed flowers and packets of letters. She put those in a box, unable to toss them out. Magazines and newspapers were easier to dispose of. She dropped those down the chute to the basement from the second floor.

Returning to the attic, she opened a trunk and found yards of draperies inside. She lifted them out and found others underneath. There were eight matching pairs, all in satin-weave material of a sunny yellow and deep apricot brocade on white.

Whitney was elated. The drapes looked as if they had been made for the living room and antechamber. She hoped so. They would add the perfect touch to the restructured area. She'd use the colors on accent pieces to brighten the rooms.

Carrying one pair of curtains, she hurried down the steps. The phone rang. She heard Gabe answer.

"Whitney, it's for you," he called out.

"Coming." It was the first time he'd used her real name. She liked the sound of it. His voice was as smooth as molasses in July, sort of dark and sexy, hinting at a sweetness yet to come.

The call was from Mr. Tall. Her order was in.

"I'll come in this afternoon," she decided.

"Is the road open?"

She glanced at Gabe with a grateful smile. "Yes." She thanked the store owner and said goodbye, then spoke to her handyman. "Would you like to ride into town this afternoon?"

He picked up the hammer. The wall studs were down, piled neatly along one side of the hall. "I'll finish the closet."

She knew better than to order him to rest. "Um, I might need some help carrying the stuff out." She assumed a worried frown. "But that might be too hard on you."

"I'll go."

A smidgen of triumph danced through her. "Do you have shoes?"

"I can get into my jogging shoes, if that's what you're asking." He limped up the stairs.

"Grouchy," she murmured. He was restless again. The drive into town would give him a change of scenery plus rest his foot.

Ten minutes later they started out. The pickup had been cleared of snow. "Nothing like having the right friends," she remarked.

Gabe didn't reply.

She turned the radio to a country-western, soft-rock station and sang along with the performers. "'I'm a stayin' kind of woman. You're a leavin' kind of man.'"

Her eyes met his in a brief melding of the minds. She turned her attention back to the road while she wondered if he thought the song matched them—she, determined to stay and live her dream, he, determined to sell out and move on.

An hour later they arrived at the town. Whitney found a parking space in front of the hardware store. She clambered out and let him do the same. Inside the store, Mr. Tall was adding up an order for someone else. Mrs. Tall sat near the stove as usual.

Whitney went back to speak to the older woman while she waited to get her wallpaper and window shades, paint and nails.

"Well, you survived the storm without mishap, it appears," Mrs. Tall greeted her.

"Yes. I haven't heard a weather report. How much snow did we get?"

"About three feet. There's more on the way."

"Really? This is breaking all records, isn't it?"

The older woman started to answer, then snapped her mouth closed, her lips thin with disapproval. Gabe entered the store, looked around and headed toward the back.

"Do you remember Gabe Deveraux?" Whitney inquired when he came near. "He's agreed to help me with the renovations."

"What about Jack Peters?" Mrs. Tall wanted to know.

"Mr. Peters decided to visit his sister in California. I wanted to get on with the job," Whitney explained, her tone cooling a bit in light of the woman's unwelcoming manner toward Gabe.

"Hello, Mrs. Tall." Gabe nodded, his expression blandly pleasant, his eyes cynically amused.

"Well, it's been a while since we've seen you around," Mrs. Tall commented, laying her knitting in her lap to study him.

"Yes," he agreed. "But I don't think anyone missed me."

Whitney groaned silently at his sardonic tone. He didn't give a darn about winning friends and influencing his neighbors.

"Your father was a hard man, but a fair one, I always heard. It broke his heart when you ran off." Mrs. Tall gave him a stern frown as she delivered this line. She held the son personally responsible, it seemed. "He was a lonely, bitter man in the end."

Whitney was immediately furious. The woman had no right to censure Gabe. She knew nothing of the relationship between father and son. "Perhaps he should have thought of that when he broke his son's heart and forced him to leave his home," Whitney put in.

Gabe laid a hard grip on her shoulder, silencing her when she would have said more. "That was a long time ago," he said quietly. "I think your order is ready," he told her.

When she glanced at him, his eyes met hers in silent fury. He was angry with her, she realized. She looked away as heat seeped upward into her face. She should have kept her mouth shut. She had no business butting in.

"Here's that wallpaper you wanted," Mr. Tall called out. "You must be going to do the whole house."

"Excuse me," she said to no one in particular, and went to the counter. She counted the rolls of paper and made sure they were the ones she'd wanted. "All the bedrooms need freshening up. This will do the trick."

She managed to smile and chat while she wrote a check for the amount, then helped the two men load the pickup. When they were ready to leave, her conscience bothered her, so she went to make her peace with Mrs. Tall.

"That sweater is so darling. I see you're almost finished." She complimented the woman on her handiwork.

"Yes, I did twelve sweaters last year," she said proudly, holding the tiny garment up. She studied Whitney for a minute. "Don't go losing your heart to that Deveraux boy," she warned in kind concern. "I'll admit he's good-looking enough to turn a girl's head, but there's bad blood there."

"He's been very helpful to me. And very nice."

"Well, he was in with a gang of thieves when he was younger. I'd be careful about having him in the house. Watch him when he comes over to work."

"He's staying at my house," Whitney said, her chin in the air. "He's been there since Saturday."

Mrs. Tall looked shocked.

Whitney knew the story would spread like wildfire now that it was out. She decided she may as well tell the whole of it. "His foot was caught in an old bear trap. I found him, took him to my place and had Dr. Payne out to see him. He has a job with me as long as he wants it."

"You may regret that. No one knows anything about him, where he's been, or what he's been doing all the time he's been gone." Mrs. Tall worked two stitches off her needles with an agitated air. "He could be an escaped convict for all we know. A thief, maybe a murderer—"

"Really, Mrs. Tall," Whitney chided as gently as she could, considering she was fuming with anger. "That kind of talk can start vicious rumors. Gabe Deveraux is honorable and good and as trustworthy as anyone I've ever—"

"Are you ready?"

Gabe's dark growl broke into her defense of his moral character. She whirled around, surprised to see him directly behind them. She realized things were not well between them by the look in his eyes.

"I'll, uh, see you later," she said to the older couple as Gabe took her arm and herded her out the door and into the cold.

The trip back to the house began in total silence. She wondered how it was going to end.

Chapter Six

Whitney's nerves were stretched to the breaking point by the time she turned into the lane, drove to the house and stopped. She glanced at Gabe. He was staring into the distance, but his mind was on an internal vista, one that excluded her.

"Don't ever do that again," he said.

She didn't pretend to misunderstand. "I can't stand by and let a friend be maligned."

"She wasn't being malicious. She was trying to warn you about taking in strangers."

"You aren't a stranger." The anger returned. "You were born and raised here."

"And had a reputation for being wild. I was the typical teenager—defiant and abrasive." He turned to her, his expression grim. "Listen, Irish, I don't need anyone to defend me. All that was a long time ago. I didn't give a damn what they thought then. And I don't give a damn now."

"But you did care." She touched his arm, feeling it was important that he understand this vulnerable side of himself. "That was why you ran away."

A muscle moved in his forearm. She felt it tense under her fingers. He didn't reply.

"Wasn't it?" she persisted softly. He moved his arm, and she drew her hand back to her side.

"Was it?" he mocked. "You seem to have all the answers."

"You were accused of theft due to circumstantial evidence. Your father...he didn't believe you when you pleaded—"

"I didn't plead for anything," he choked out.

"When you said you had nothing to do with it," she amended her statement. "*That* was the real reason you left." She studied him, her gaze tender and full of sympathy. "Wasn't it?"

His face was impassive when he answered. "Yes. Would you like to know the rest of it...that he took his belt off and beat me with the buckle until my back was a solid welt of bruises...that he cursed and disowned me...that I stood there, defiant to the end, refusing to speak...that we never spoke again?" He thrust the door open and slid out of the truck.

Tears pressed against her eyes, hot with anguish for the boy who'd been hurt clear to his soul. He'd never gotten over that betrayal. She shook her head, unable to speak.

He glanced back at her. "Save your tears," he advised harshly. "You'll need them when your heart is trampled by those you trust. Mrs. Tall was right to warn you. You don't know a damn thing about me or the life I've lived."

"Yes, I do."

"I've done things, Irish, that would shock you right out of your Puritan little mind," he told her with a cruel smile. "You would do better to guard yourself than to defend me."

Giving the door a slam, he grabbed two bags from the truck bed and walked into the house, his limp evident as he ignored the pain and increased his stride.

Whitney sat there behind the wheel and gazed out at the snow-covered mountains that rose all around the narrow valley. Warm sunshine poured into the truck, but her heart felt cold. In spite of his warning about being tender-hearted, she worried about him and the injustices in his past.

The townspeople, without proof, much less a conviction, had decided he was a thief. His own father—the one person who should have known him well enough to stand beside him—hadn't believed in his innocence. Thus, Gabe had discarded his trust in others and made his own way in life.

Whitney understood the anguish now, and the deep well of bitterness within him. Somehow she had to help him overcome it.

Gabe Deveraux had a great deal of love to give to some lucky woman. It would be terrible if he never knew the full potential within himself and what it could mean to another person.

"You're special," she whispered to his restless spirit. "You're special to *me*."

She sighed shakily. For the first time she thought falling in love might be worth the risk. A sinking feeling in her middle told her what her heart had known for ages. She had no choice in the matter. She was already in love with Gabe.

Whitney pressed her hands in the small of her back and stretched her weary muscles. There, the wall in the office alcove under the stairs was done. She closed the bucket of wallpaper paste, then went into the bathroom to wash the brush she'd used to spread the paste.

The telephone rang.

She dried her hands and returned to the alcove. The phone was on the lowest step. She sat down, her back to the wall, and picked it up. "Hello?" With one hand, she untied her shoelaces and slipped off her sneakers. Her feet were tired.

"Let me speak to Deveraux, please," a man's voice, impatient and abrupt, requested.

Expecting to hear from her mother, it took Whitney a second to collect herself. "I'll get him."

"Right."

She resisted the urge to ask who was calling. Instead she put the receiver on the stair runner and padded down the hall in her socks, stopping abruptly at the door to her room.

Gabe was standing on the very top of her five-foot ladder, putting the shades she'd purchased on the fourteen-foot window.

Alarms went off inside her. She didn't speak, afraid she'd surprise him into a sudden move. While she watched, he stretched his arms up and positioned one end of the rod, then leaned the other way and fastened the other end.

Keeping one hand on the window frame for balance, he drew the shade down with him as he stepped down one rung.

He froze in place.

Her heart leapt to her throat.

She saw him shift his weight to his good foot, then he swung his head around until he was looking at her. Every movement was slow and calculated. His eyes raked down her, paused at her sock-clad feet, then returned to her face.

It was like being touched all over.

"Yes?" he said.

"You... you shouldn't stand up there," she said, coming out of her trance. "It's too dangerous. You could fall." She hurried to the ladder and grabbed it from the side while he climbed down. "There's another ladder in the basement. It's taller."

"I saw it." He leveled the edge of the window shade with the midpoint of the window.

"Then why didn't you use it?" she snapped, glaring up at him.

"This one was handy. Did you want something in particular, or did you just come in to yell at me?"

She remembered why she was there. "You have a call."

He frowned. "Why didn't you say so?" He hurried across the room and up the hall to the stairs.

Whitney examined her room. It looked much better.

She'd washed the windows on the inside first thing that morning—she'd worry about the outside in the spring when the weather improved—and Gabe had installed the new shades at the four windows. Now she'd have privacy at night.

In addition, he'd helped her carry her unpacked boxes to a small room behind the kitchen, then they'd arranged her living and bedroom furniture exactly where she'd wanted it. The large bedroom would be her private sitting room when she got the B&B to running.

She'd found the telephone from her apartment as well as the answering machine. They were now plugged in and ready for use in the kitchen planning area.

Although it was early, she decided to call it a day. Gabe had been on his feet most of the afternoon. Getting her flannel gown from a drawer, she headed for the shower.

Gabe's voice rose as she stepped into the hall. "Last night? In the storm? Pretty damn good," he remarked with a cynical laugh.

She paused, but didn't hear anything else when he dropped back to a murmur. She wondered what had happened and who he was talking to. Other than the resort owner, he didn't claim any friends.

Going into the bathroom, she closed the door behind her and stripped out of her clothes. In the shower, her mind ran in endless circles of speculation about her mysterious handyman.

When she came out in her gown and robe, Gabe was in her room, laying a fire in the grate. "You're quitting early tonight."

"Uh-huh. I'm tired." She glanced down the lean, powerful length of him. "You must be, too. You shouldn't be on your foot so much."

He shrugged carelessly. His mind wasn't on his health. She saw his gaze flick to the window and the silhouette of the trees and buildings on his ranch in the last light of evening. He stood.

She moved aside when he came to the door. "Are you going to shower now? I thought I'd prepare an early supper."

He hesitated. "All right."

While he cleaned up, she stir-fried chicken breasts with herbs and served the cubed pieces over spinach noodles. A large bowl of fresh fruit salad and whole wheat rolls accompanied the simple meal. She looked at the table and chairs that they'd moved to the corner of the kitchen, then loaded the food onto a tray.

She carried the tray to her room and set it on the coffee table. After setting up two TV tables, she placed plates, napkins and flatware on them, then went back for a pot of tea. Hearing the water go off, she glanced up the stairs.

A picture of him in her shower leapt full-blown into her mind. He had lifted her into the bathtub as if she were a featherweight. He'd cupped her breast through her wet gown. Warmth coursed through her, and her nipple beaded, eager for more of his touch.

On the way back with the tea things, she heard a door open, then another open and close. He must be in the room he'd chosen for his bedroom.

In a few minutes he entered her quarters. He wore a clean, blue sweatshirt and stone-washed jeans. She'd washed those clothes with hers. The atmosphere seemed suddenly intimate.

She took a seat on the small sofa.

"Sit in the chair," he said, coming to the sitting area.

"No, this is fine." She thought the chair would be more comfortable for him.

"I want to prop my foot up," he told her.

She glanced down at his foot, now enclosed in the soft splint. She leapt up. "Is your ankle still swollen?"

"Some. I . . . may have been on it too much today."

The admission surprised her. She realized he was waiting for her to sit before he did. She slipped into her favorite chair.

He settled into the corner of the sofa and stretched his injured foot down its length. "How about turning on the news? I haven't heard what's happening in the world in days."

She flicked on the TV. While they ate and listened to the world news, she mulled over the time he'd been there. He'd been injured on Tuesday. She'd found him on Wednesday. Today was Sunday. Five days, yet she felt she'd known him a lifetime.

When the local news came on, she noticed a frown nick twin lines between his eyes. He suddenly seemed more intent. She flicked her attention to the television.

"The warehouse was stripped of equipment that was valued at half a million dollars," the local news anchor said. "Carly Lightfoot is at the scene with the police report."

The camera switched to an outdoor location. Several police cars were parked at haphazard angles in front of a warehouse. A yellow crime tape stretched across the open bay of the building. People moved busily around inside. A tall man in a uniform, wearing a black Stetson, bent under the tape and emerged.

"There's the sheriff," the reporter said. She called out to him. He stopped and waited for her to catch up. The camera focused on the rugged features of the county sheriff.

Questions and answers were exchanged. The sheriff's replies were brief and to the point. "We have no clues to the identity of the perpetrators," he said, his handsome face unsmiling. "The state patrol is working with us."

His brusque manner and deep voice plucked a chord in Whitney's memory. She'd heard that same tone and inflection a short time ago...when the call came for Gabe.

"He questioned you, didn't he?" she said in a tight, furious voice. She clenched her hands in frustrated anger.

Gabe raised one dark eyebrow.

"The sheriff. He was the one who called earlier." Her anger increased. "They always suspect someone who's been in trouble in the past. Did he want to know if you had an alibi last night?"

"You've been watching too many TV shows," Gabe said.

"You were here all night. I can vouch for that."

His hand tightened on the knife he held to butter the roll. "Thanks," he drawled. "If anyone asks, I'll refer them to you." His dark eyes stayed on the television screen as he made light of her intuitive guess.

Then he looked at her.

There was fire and passion in his gaze, and an intensity that couldn't be disguised by his sardonic manner. Again she was drawn inside...deep...deeper...until she felt she could touch his soul.

She realized she had. Her anger on his behalf had moved him, whether he admitted it or not. Suddenly her heart was singing.

The news changed to the weather. He released her from the captivity of his gaze. His expression became remote. The moment of communication might never have been.

And might never be again, she realized. Gabe wanted her, was drawn to her for more than physical passion, but he'd held himself aloof from others for years. He might never trust again.

After the meal, he went to his room, which was upstairs and on the opposite side of the house from hers. Later, after she lay in bed, restless and unfulfilled, she heard the creak of timber above her head. She tensed, knowing he was in the bedroom directly above hers rather than his own.

Was he watching his ranch and thinking of long-ago days when his mother had been alive and he'd been happy?

She didn't know if he'd ever known joy, but surely he had. Surely there had been days when he'd raced across green fields with all the ardor of a youthful heart, glad to be alive.

But that had been long ago, and now he watched, dark and brooding, for... something.

A premonition of danger washed over her like clumps of snow falling abruptly from a tree, chilling her through and through. Gabe had returned home for a reason. She wanted to know what it was.

"That looks very nice," the salesclerk said. "Blue works wonderfully with your eyes."

Whitney turned this way and that in front of the mirrors. The conservative blue dress wasn't quite right. She could wear one of the business suits she'd worn to work in Washington just as well.

Sighing, she shook her head. "I think I'll look some more."

She changed back to her jeans and sweater, slipped into her sneakers and stuck her high heels in a shopping bag. She'd been unable to find an outfit in Riverton or Medford. She'd been sure she'd find something in Ashland. No such luck.

Gabe was standing in front of the store when she went out. He was studying the displays in the windows like a design student preparing for an exam.

Heat seeped into her face as she wondered if he'd seen her in the various outfits the clerk had urged her to try. Some of them had been ridiculous—like that lace and velvet confection in mauve. She'd looked like a scrawny chicken, one of the Rhode Island Reds her grandmother used to keep.

"Ready?" she asked, the word coming out impatient and angry.

He nodded. He turned and went to the truck, taking the driver's side. He walked in long, coordinated strides, with no discernible limp. An athlete's walk.

It was the third week in January, sixteen days since he'd been injured. He seemed to have recovered with no problem.

Tomorrow was Friday, the date for the Riverton Chamber of Commerce Winter Follies. She'd wanted something special to wear.

Her gaze was drawn irresistibly to Gabe. All right, so she'd wanted him to see her in something besides jeans or sweats. She stared at the scenery on the long ride home.

He flicked her a glance, then looked back at the road as they turned into the lane leading to the house. Each time their eyes met, something happened inside her. Electricity jolted along her nerves, and her heart seemed to stop, then beat furiously.

She was acting like a hormone-racked adolescent, she scolded. The reprimand did no good. *Mind-blowing*, that's how he'd said it would be if they ever made love.

Heat rushed through her. Her heart beat like mad.

She looked at the melting snow under the trees. Even snow wouldn't calm her wild longings. She would be twenty-eight in April. She wanted to throw caution to the winds and know fulfillment.

Which would be stupid. Where was the common sense that usually guided her?

At the house, she and Gabe got out of the truck and started unloading the supplies. He got the heavy stuff, such as the new stainless-steel sink for the kitchen. She carried in the bags of groceries, then returned for the sets of sheets, a different color for each bedroom, to match the wallpaper she'd put up.

It was dark by the time Gabe had the new sink installed. The new commercial-size stove was already in place. An upright freezer hummed alongside the refrigerator. The kitchen was ready for business.

She prepared sandwiches for supper. "What are you going to wear tomorrow night?" she asked when they were seated at the small table they'd moved to the kitchen breakfast nook.

He looked at her as if she'd asked a very personal question. A picture of him in her bed, wearing her extra-large T-shirt, came to her. Then she pictured him as he'd been in the shower, wearing nothing. Her breasts tingled as she recalled his touch through the wet, clinging flannel.

She cleared her throat. "I meant, to the dance."

"I hadn't planned on going."

"You have to." She gave him an annoyed glance. The Winter Follies fitted in her plan to reintroduce him to the community, and the community to him.

"Is that an order?" His face was expressionless, but there was turbulence in his eyes as he challenged her authority.

"No, of course not," she murmured. "I just thought... Well, it doesn't matter." She struggled to hide her disappointment. It hadn't occurred to her that he wouldn't go.

"I'm not staying here, so there's no reason for me to cozy up to the local citizens."

She lost interest in attending.

"You, on the other hand, have every reason," he continued as if reading her thoughts. "Goodwill is important in business. Local merchants will refer travelers to your place, but only if they know and like you. *You* have to be sociable. I don't."

She worried about him, off in the world by himself, no one to care if he lived or died. A person would take unnecessary risks in situations like that. "Where will you go when you leave here?" she asked, her voice going soft.

Gabe heard the concern she tried to hide behind a nonchalant front. More than once, he'd seen her studying him, her blue eyes dark with worry. It gave him the strangest sensation behind his breastbone. As if he were being punched from the inside.

"Don't worry about me," he told her, his tone sharper than he'd meant. The natural blush in her cheeks deepened. He felt like a heel.

Her chin came up. "I don't. Why should I?"

Liar. He didn't say it. The word would have come out as a caress rather than a reprimand. He didn't know how much longer he could maintain a cool distance between them.

At night he lay in bed and thought about the way she'd cared for him when he was hurt. With no thought to her own safety, she'd taken him into her home...put him in her *bed*, for Pete's sake, and then, to top it all off, had given him a job and taken his side against the town gossip. That did things to a man.

Things he couldn't afford to let affect him, he reminded himself harshly. So he was attracted to her...and her to him. That was natural. The sex drive was one of the strongest drives in nature, and she was one of the sexiest women he'd ever run across in all his travels.

He shook his head, trying to dislodge the images of her that formed in his mind...like that night in the shower. For a moment, induced by the concussion, he'd thought she was his, that she'd come to him, offering him love and peace and contentment.

The stupid fantasy of a mixed-up mind, that was all it was. He had other plans—a job to do, a career to return to, a world to see. He ignored the snide voice inside that reminded him that he'd already seen most of the world and hadn't been terribly impressed.

A home, the thought came to him. It had been a long time since he'd had a home. He still didn't. He was here to stop the thieves using the ranch, clear his name, then sell the damn place. That was all.

Grimly, he finished the meal, excused himself and went to his room. It was going to be a long night...one of many.

Whitney listened to the faint sounds of pacing over her head. Gabe was growing more restless every day. His moods were darker, his suppressed anger almost palpable. She knew with certainty that he would be leaving soon. She wondered what he was waiting for.

A tiny fear crept into her. Half a million dollars in stolen equipment? Was that why he stayed?

Her heart refused to believe it. She turned over in bed, pulled the cord to raise the shade a bit and gazed out the window toward the ranch. A flash of light winked on, then off.

Every cell in her body jerked to attention. She lay still and stared out at the inky blackness, waiting for another flash.

She realized the house had gone very quiet as if it, too, were waiting. The faint creak of timber above her had stopped. Gabe was no longer moving about.

Ten minutes passed. No further activity was seen from the ranch. Slowly, she relaxed. Just as she drifted into sleep, she heard the almost noiseless closing of a door, then the embers in the fireplace flared as a draft swept down the hall.

Whitney flung the covers back and ran down the hall to the front door. The moon was half-full, faintly illuminating the drifts of snow on the meadow. A moving shadow was briefly visible, then it disappeared behind a tree. She watched for it to emerge, but it didn't.

In a few minutes she realized she was shivering as frosty air circulated under her gown. Her feet ached with cold. She ran back to bed. It was well past midnight when she felt the draft as the front door was opened and closed. A stair creaked a second later.

She stared at the dark ceiling and wondered where he'd been and who he'd met. A chill ran over her. She huddled deeper into the covers, her heart as cold as a boulder in the field.

It was late when Whitney woke up. The sun was already over the horizon, a sliver of gold in the pale blue morning sky.

She rose, washed and dressed, aware of a weariness that was more than one of the body. She'd wrestled with her thoughts all night, unable to believe evil of Gabe.

The questions roamed uneasily through her mind. Mysterious lights, a midnight jaunt into the dark...

Gabe was at the table when she entered the kitchen. She searched his face for signs of his sleepless night. He looked fit and fresh. Resentment stirred in her.

"Good morning," he said quietly over a cup of coffee.

"Good morning." She poured a cup and leaned against the counter, blowing across the steaming liquid before drinking.

"What is it?"

"Nothing."

He looked irritated. "Come on, Irish, say whatever's on your mind. I don't want to be the recipient of dirty looks all day without knowing the cause. I know how you women operate."

Her temper flared. She slammed the cup down. "What about how you men operate?" she demanded.

"Such as?" He was cool, controlled.

She waved a hand and pointed toward the west. "Such as going off into the night to check on your ranch. Didn't you ever stop to think the crooks might be on the lookout, ready to finish off anyone who got in their way?"

He hesitated, then said, "Yeah, that occurred to me."

His laconic answer sent her blood pressure into the danger zone. "But you just had to dash over when you saw a light—"

"What do you know about a light?" The quietness of his tone shocked her out of her tirade. He looked dangerous, like a cat waiting to attack.

"I saw it from my bedroom."

"You were supposed to pull the shades at night," he reminded her. "That's why I put the damned things up."

"I did." At his unrelenting gaze, she hastened to explain. "I...had trouble sleeping, so I raised one to look...to look at the moonlight." She sounded as defensive as a teenager caught coming in after curfew.

"What else did you see?"

"I saw you going across the meadow."

The silence was ominous.

"You could have been hurt," she began, then stopped, knowing it was too late. She'd already laid her heart bare in her worry over him.

He set the cup down and stood. "Don't ever spy on me again," he said in a strained tone she'd never heard from him.

She dared to meet his eyes. There was anger in them, but it didn't frighten her. She sensed a struggle going on in him, and saw a wild surge of emotion that she couldn't read.

"I wasn't spying," she said with a quiet dignity of her own. "I was concerned for your safety. Without cause, it seems."

His dark gaze drilled into her. "Without cause?"

She drew a determined breath. "Perhaps you weren't in danger, at all. Perhaps you were going over to meet your contacts."

Invisible forces strummed in the air between them. "Is that what you think?"

"No. I don't know." Her fingers trembled on the cup. She held it tighter. "I guess I'm asking why you'd go off into the night after being hurt so recently..." Her voice trailed off into a question. She waited for the fury to break over her.

His hand clenched until his knuckles gleamed whiter than the mug he gripped. "Would you believe me if I told you?" he asked with a cynical half smile curling his lips.

She hated it when he became closed and taunting, as if he knew that nothing he said would make a difference.

"Yes."

"Just like that?" he mocked.

She realized he didn't trust her. But why should he, she demanded, when the people who had watched him grow up had hurt him with their distrust? Why should he take her word?

"Just like that," she agreed, smiling slightly. "I think you went over to investigate whoever was on your property. I want you to tell me if that was the reason."

"Do you think I'd admit it if I went over for other purposes, such as to claim my share of a half-million-dollar haul?"

That was a hard one to answer. "I'd know if you were lying," she finally said.

She wondered if she was being the biggest fool on the entire earth, but the fact was, she'd accept whatever he told her. She simply couldn't believe he'd lie to her. "I've looked into your soul, and I know it's... good."

The word was inadequate, but it was the best she could come up with. Maybe he wasn't *pure*, but he was a good man. She'd stake her life on it.

It came to her that she might be doing just that.

He shook his head. "You're either the wisest woman on earth, or the dumbest, Irish. It would be a toss-up to decide between the two."

"Thanks." She returned his sardonic half smile. It didn't take a prophet to see he wasn't going to answer her. "Would you like waffles for breakfast?" she asked, turning from him. "I found my grandmother's waffle iron. Or I can fix some eggs, if you'd rather have them."

"Waffles," he answered. He left the kitchen.

She noticed he limped slightly. He had probably overtired his ankle with that trek across the snow, or perhaps turned it. In the dark, shadows could be tricky. She prepared the waffle mix, her mind only half on the task.

Fear reached deep inside her. Men who stole half a million dollars' worth of goods would probably shoot an intruder on sight. Gabe, in defending his home, would wade right into them.

She stopped stirring the batter as the truth hit her. Gabe had found out his ranch was being used for illegal purposes and had returned home to stop it. Once before, his name had been blackened by thieves. He wasn't going to allow it to happen again.

Realizing this also let her see that he had answered her... in his own fashion. By going against popular opinion and taking his side, she would be the wise one in the community if he were honest and only she saw it. She would end up the fool, though, if he weren't.

She wondered which she was. Only Gabe's actions would prove that.

But, she fretted, in confronting the crooks, he might get hurt. Worse, he might be accused of being one of them. If the investigators found stolen goods on his property, he could be in serious trouble.

Of course she would vouch for his honesty, and that he had been in the house until the light had indicated someone was at the ranch. But she'd have to admit he'd gone out.

She remembered the sense of purpose about him when he'd stood under the trees at the boundary between their places. She'd thought he was a man with a mission. She still did.

When he returned with the toolbox, she was under control. Whatever events were under way, they would have to play out in their own time. She'd wait and see what happened.

"I'll sort the stuff in the basement. What are your plans?" He sounded quite amiable, as if he hadn't been furious only moments ago.

"I'm going to start painting the living room and antechamber."

"I'll help you as soon as I finish in here."

She nodded.

Chapter Seven

Whitney stood in front of the closet. She looked at her business suits, most of them with pants rather than skirts. They didn't please her. She looked at the two cocktail dresses she'd bought for her mother's social affairs. They were too . . . simple.

Hesitantly, she took out the dress her mother had given her for Christmas. It was black, much too short and had two rows of net ruffling at the hem. The bodice was like a strapless gown, but again, silk netting, called French Illusion, had been utilized for the yoke and sleeves. This gave the dress a facade of modesty when, in effect, it was very provocative.

"Wear it," a deep male voice told her.

She swung around. Gabe stood in the doorway, his tall, muscular body filling it as he leaned against the frame. His thumbs were hooked into his jeans' back pockets. His stance was casual, yet he had a certain primal attractiveness that had probably broken wiser hearts than hers.

"It's too . . . too . . ." She couldn't think of the term.

"Flirty?" he suggested in a low, throaty drawl that strummed across her heart strings like the bow of a violin. He smiled.

His teeth gleamed white against the swarthy tan of his face. His eyes crinkled at the corners as he challenged her to wear the daring outfit.

"Sort of. For Riverton. Don't you think?" She hated that she sounded so unsure of herself. After all, she'd attended her mother's receptions for years . . . and had sat quietly in the background like one of the rented palms. For once in her life, she wanted to attract a man . . . a special man.

"Riverton is pretty sophisticated these days, what with the ski crowd and the artsy folks passing through."

"Well, maybe." She didn't say she would; she didn't say she wouldn't. She'd make up her mind after supper and a shower.

"Here." He tossed an object to her.

She caught it. Holding the container up, she read the name on front. "Henna?" She looked at him with a questioning glance.

A red tint seemed to creep into his cheeks. "I was . . . um, visiting in the Mideast once. The women there use henna. I thought you might like to try it."

"All right." She wasn't too sure about using the stuff. Her hair had plenty of red highlights. That was the problem with it, in her opinion. She read the instructions. "I'll put it on now."

She got a towel and went into the kitchen. Using a stainless-steel mixing bowl, she emptied the container. Henna, she found, looked like dried, powdered leaves. Green leaves.

After making a paste of hot water and henna, she wet her hair and rubbed the mixture over the long strands. She decided to let it stay on for forty minutes, on the theory that it would take a lot of time to subdue the carroty tints in her natural hair.

If her hair came out green, she'd pretend she'd done it as a conversation piece for the occasion. And if they believed that, she'd offer them this bridge she had for sale....

After writing a letter to her best friend back in Washington, she prepared supper, feeling silly with a shower cap over her head to keep the henna paste from dripping.

"Very fetching," Gabe commented with a smile, taking his seat at the table after she called him to eat. She'd made grilled ham-and-cheese sandwiches with a plate of fresh vegetables alongside.

The teasing light in his eyes warmed and surprised her. "You should smile more often," she told him.

The smile disappeared. "Yeah."

"No, really. You're very handsome when you smile. Not that you aren't when you don't smile," she hastened to add, "but...when you do...it's...you look so..." She stopped and frowned. "You get me flustered. I've never had that problem before."

Because the guys in college had been just that—guys she studied with, played cards with. They weren't potential lovers.

And Gabe was?

She wasn't sure. There was an undercurrent of desire that ran between them constantly. It was unnerving... exciting... fraught with uncertainty.

"Passion can be pretty daunting," he murmured. "Especially if you've never tried it before."

"There's always a first time." She couldn't believe she'd said that. Provocative statements weren't her way. She was too straightforward to play those kinds of games; at least, she used to be.

He chuckled, bringing her gaze to his. "Watch it, Irish. I might take you up on that offer."

"I didn't...did I make an offer?" She wasn't sure if they were joking or not.

He didn't answer. Picking up his sandwich, he ate without further discussion. She wished she could think of something to lure him into conversation again. Her mother could chatter on for ages in that appealing way she had, but Whitney had thought all that sort of thing silly. She wished she'd listened now.

"It's almost six," Gabe reminded her.

She nodded and finished eating quickly. She put her dishes in the dishwasher and dashed to the bathroom. There, she rinsed the paste out of her hair, finished bathing and dried off. With a towel around her head and wearing the terry cloth robe, she dashed into her room to finish dressing.

While pulling on sheer black stockings, she heard the shower come on in the upstairs bathroom. It would be such fun if Gabe were to come with her. Her entire body tingled at the thought of going out with him. And then coming home with him later... just the two of them.

She glanced at the bed. She'd hardly slept the night he'd been in it. She'd been too worried about his injuries. That wouldn't be a problem now. He was well enough...

Taking a deep breath, she stopped the useless thoughts. He didn't want involvement of any kind.

After spritzing cologne around her shoulders, she slipped into black underclothes, then the dress and black patent-leather pumps. She hurried back to the bathroom where she spent an impatient ten minutes drying her long hair. Really, she should have it cut.

Finished, she pinned the wild mass on top of her head by twisting it and sticking a Japanese pick of black-and-gold enamel through the center of the twist. Leaning toward the tiny mirror over the sink to put on her makeup, she blinked in surprise.

Her hair was different. Gone was the brassy tone. In its place was a softly glowing auburn, a shade brighter than her grandmother's had been, but still, it was very nice.

Pleased, she looked at it from every angle before putting on a light dusting of makeup. She rushed back to her room. It was time for her to be on the road. She'd go into town, mingle with the crowd, then come home early.

She found her good purse, then grabbed her warm parka from the closet. She glanced into the full-length mirror mounted on the inside of the door. Her mouth dropped open.

The black silk hugged her body until it ended in the flirty ruffle midway down her thighs. The ruffle added interest to her otherwise slender silhouette, bringing the eyes past her hips to linger on her legs. There was something scandalously provocative about that ruffled flounce.

The top was worse. It was blatantly sexy. The sheer silk covered her arms and shoulders, showing a hint of cleavage—she didn't have a lot of that—without hiding anything. The bodice demurely shielded her breasts from view, but not their shape.

There was no way she was going to her first formal meeting with the other business people in town looking like a . . . a . . . well, something she wasn't. She reached for the zipper. Her blue suit would have to do.

"Wear it."

She turned from the mirror. Gabe lounged in the doorway again, observing her. He wore a dark suit with a light blue shirt and black tie. Her eyes widened as she took in his appearance. "You're going?" she asked, dazed by his tall, masculine splendor.

He nodded. "The roads might be icy when you come home." That was all he said by way of explanation.

A glow crept over her, seeping from deep inside until she could feel it in her skin, radiating heat like a stove.

She looked at her reflection. "It's—"

"Perfect," he interrupted. He came over and stood behind her. The top of her head was level with his lips in her evening shoes. Just right for dancing together.

"Don't you think it's too—"

Again he didn't wait for her to finish. "No." He held her parka for her, then turned her and zipped it to her neck. "You'd better wear your boots and carry your shoes."

She slipped out of her pumps and pulled on socks and the insulated boots. When she was ready, she saw he was, too. He carried his black parka and an afghan over his arm.

Picking up her shoes, he escorted her to the truck and lifted her in, then covered her legs with the afghan.

She felt fragile next to his great strength. And, even more strange, she felt cherished by his gentle care.

On the drive to town, she couldn't stop staring at him. His stern, rather forbidding expression didn't deter her imagination one bit. She was wildly, romantically, passionately in love for the first time in her life. Nothing could change that.

Gabe cursed silently as he parked the truck next to the community center. He shouldn't have come. The temptation was too great. Hell, he was only a man, not a saint.

He tried to ease the scowl from his face as he got out to help Whitney down. Instead of lifting her out, he took her hand to steady her as she jumped to the ground. He was aware of her quick look before she turned determinedly toward the light spilling from the open door as other couples went in.

He confused her with his changes of mood. He knew that. It couldn't be helped. He tried to ignore the passion between them, but sometimes it was hard. Sometimes it was impossible. Like tonight. No. He was there to keep an eye on her, that was all. Passion had no place in his scheme of things.

But she was so beautiful, he'd had to tag along. Some jealous female might make some catty remark. Or some local Lothario might come on to Whitney and refuse to take no for an answer. There were men like that. And it was a long, lonely trip back to the house.

That was why he'd decided to attend the damn dance.

"Hello! Come in!" the mayor called to them in his foghorn voice. "Hang your coats over there. Cold tonight, huh? Go warm yourselves by the fire. There're several young people there."

Whitney smiled and spoke to the man and his wife. She pulled Gabe to her side and introduced him. "His father owned the ranch next to my grandmother's place, you may recall."

He saw the speculation flash through the other couple's eyes as they obviously remembered him and the circumstances of his leaving. Memories were long in small towns.

For Whitney's sake, Gabe smiled and forced a cordiality he didn't feel. He wouldn't embarrass her. After moving down the reception line, they hung up their coats. She changed to her pumps, and they mingled with the local denizens. He was surprised at the number of people she knew.

An odd thing kept happening. Like a kid in the throes of his first big love, funny little jolts of electricity ran through him whenever she looked his way. He realized she was proud to be with him, as if he were a prize catch or some damn thing.

"Gabe owns the ranch next to my B&B," she said to someone whose name he vaguely recalled. As if it were a million-acre spread with a castle for a house instead of the grim reality.

Across the room, a pair of gray eyes caught his attention. The sheriff, Shane Macklin, smiled, then flicked a glance at Whitney, a question in his eyes when he looked back at Gabe.

Macklin had been a classmate of his before Gabe had struck off on his own. It had surprised the hell out of him to find that the man was now the county sheriff. The Macklin family still owned the Rogue River Orchards and was the most powerful influence in the area. The younger brother ran the business while Shane ran the county, it appeared.

Gabe gave an almost imperceptible nod to the sheriff and ignored the question in the man's eyes about his presence there. So much for his laying low and staying out of sight to not arouse suspicion about his being in the area.

What difference did it make? he argued with himself. It was bound to get out sooner or later that he had returned. The thieves would know soon enough. The noose was tightening on them. Soon he'd be free to leave this place forever.

Whitney's laughter drew him back to the present, and a pang echoed through him. He'd miss his redheaded charm when he left. He frowned at the admission, then put his mind to getting through the evening without coming unglued.

The gentle pressure of her hand on his arm guided him along. She introduced herself, then him, to another group of people.

Her cologne wafted around him, surrounding him in her scent. His mind went hazy with feelings buried for so long he didn't even know what to call them. They caused an ache inside. He knew a lot about that. Trusting anyone, getting involved . . . those hurt.

The music started. He felt Whitney's quick glance before she continued her conversation with the local feed-store owner. He set his jaw. He was *not* going to dance.

The younger couples and quite a few older ones moved onto the dance floor. Everyone else crowded to the sides.

He and Whitney were left standing with the dancers. He realized there was no hope for it. He took her into his arms.

She didn't say a word, just sort of snuggled against him as if that's where she belonged. Her head was just at the right height to rest his cheek on her temple . . . if he was of a mind for that kind of thing.

He wasn't.

Apparently she was. She moved in close. The next thing he knew, her cheek was on his shoulder. The soft warmth of her almost made his knees weak. He wanted her so much he would have given ten years off his life to possess her.

"You're like a flame," he murmured, bending his head down to hers. "You burn away a man's good sense."

"Do we have to be sensible tonight?"

When she looked at him, the sensation of drowning in her blue eyes was too real to be ignored. Going once…twice…

"Yes," he said.

"I wish . . ." She let the thought trail into silence.

But there was no need for words. He could see what she wished. Her desire for him was as great as his for her. Only she wanted things to go along with it. Like promises. And commitment. Marriage. Kids.

What did he have to offer a woman like her?

He had money, lots of it. A few lucky poker games, a natural gas strike with an honest partner and a dangerous job with Uncle Sam that paid well had taken care of his finances. With the money, he could offer a tainted name, a suspicious past and a questionable future. Yeah, he was quite a catch for any woman. . . .

He looked at Whitney. She gazed at him with her eyes full of trust and passion, just waiting to be shared with him.

No one had ever looked at him like that but her. It tore his heart out. "There's no way," he warned.

"There must be," she said simply.

He shook his head. "I'm not sticking around, Irish. It's like the song says... 'You're a staying kind of woman. I'm a leaving kind of man.'"

The pain in her eyes was haunting. She lowered her lashes, but he knew he'd see it again...and again...and again...in all the lonely dreams of a thousand lonely nights.

Ah, Irish, if only it were possible.

Damn, she'd have him believing in happily-ever-after if he didn't watch it.

"I understand." She smiled at him.

Her mouth trembled, and it was all he could do not to kiss her until they both melted.

"Don't look at me like that," he growled savagely. "Don't wear your heart on your sleeve. No man is worth it."

"You are," Whitney said. Casting her own pride aside, she spoke as truthfully as she could. "Love is worth the risk. It gives meaning to everything else. It can change disappointment into triumph. But you have to believe, Gabe. You have to be willing to take a chance."

He crushed her to him, his arm like a vise across her waist. "All right," he murmured hoarsely. "If you say so, then I believe it. It's just that it isn't for me. Not now."

She pulled away to study his expression. "Why?"

"Because things are difficult at the moment," he told her, his tone harsher. "I can't afford to be distracted."

"Your ranch," she promptly said, seeing a connection between his problems and the derelict place. "Something is happening there. You're trying to find out what."

He frowned and released his grip on her. With a respectable three inches between them, he nodded slowly. "You see too much."

When the dance ended, he escorted her to the side near the refreshment table. A woman moved over to give them room.

"Gabe!" the woman said in surprise.

Whitney quickly noted that the woman was beautiful. She had black hair and green eyes. There were a few freckles sprinkled attractively across her nose.

"Genny," he said, his manner warm as if he were pleased to see her. He introduced the women. "Whitney is a neighbor," he explained. "She's also my...um, current employer."

Whitney noted he wasn't as surprised to see the woman as she was to see him, and that he hesitated in mentioning his job.

After saying hello and giving Whitney a warm smile, Genny turned back to Gabe. "What are you doing in these parts? I thought you'd be long gone by now."

"I'm thinking of selling the ranch," he said.

Whitney noted that he didn't make it definite. Perhaps he had changed his mind since he'd told her he was going to sell. Her heart gave an excited little leap in her chest.

"You'd sell your home?" the woman questioned. "Everyone needs a place to come back to."

Whitney met his quick glance. A sardonic smile curled the corners of his mouth. "So I've been told." He looked over the crowd. "Where's Rafe?"

"The men's room. Maybe you'd better go check on him. He's been gone awhile."

"He's probably arguing with someone over the business prospects of the community," Gabe decided. "I'll scout him out and bring him back." He left them and threaded his way across the noisy room.

Nearby, a hushed whisper reached her ears as one woman exclaimed to another, "Look, isn't that Gabe Deveraux?"

"Huh," her friend said with a sniff. "I never thought he'd come back to these parts. He didn't bother to show up for his own father's funeral."

"I heard his father ran him off..."

Whitney clenched her hands to keep from lashing out at the women as they walked past her and out of hearing.

Gabe *had* returned when his father died. Maybe he hadn't gotten back for the funeral—or maybe he hadn't wanted to deal with people who stared at him and gossiped about him behind his back, she wanted to tell them—but if they'd seen his grief, they'd have known how wrong they were.

"So you're a neighbor of Gabe's?" the woman Gabe had called Genny asked with a friendly smile.

"Yes," she said. "I'm going to open a bed-and-breakfast inn, to catch the overflow from the resort, I hope. Gabe is staying at my place while he's helping with the work." She didn't know why she'd added this last bit of information.

Genny seemed glad that he was employed. "Hmm, that's good. I wonder... well, never mind." Her smile was oddly mysterious. "He did some work at the resort, too, clearing the paths of snow, that sort of thing. Ask him to tell you about it sometime."

Whitney felt there was more to that suggestion than met the ear, so to speak, but she hadn't a clue as to what it could be. A frisson crept down her spine like a slowly melting icicle.

Before she could question the woman further, Gabe and another man appeared at the doorway leading to the hall. They both halted and looked over the room before edging around the dancers and coming to her and Genny.

That tiny pause alarmed Whitney. There was a wariness in both men, a sense of caution learned somewhere other than a small valley in southern Oregon. Gabe might have worked for Rafe at the resort, but they'd known each other at some other place, in some other circumstances, during a time of danger.

The appearance of a third man at the doorway brought her gaze back to there. The sheriff stopped and leaned his shoulder against the frame with a casual air, but his gaze, like that of the other two men, was wary as it roamed the crowded room. His narrow-eyed scrutiny reminded Whitney of a predator, one who was on the prowl.

Fear ate at her while she tried to chat and smile in an amiable manner when Gabe introduced her to Rafe Barrett, the owner of the resort, who was rather more than a past employer, it seemed.

She was aware of the tension Gabe hid very effectively from the others. If she hadn't been attuned to his every nuance, she wouldn't have caught it, either.

Had the sheriff stopped Gabe and questioned him about activities at his ranch? What if the stolen goods were discovered there and Gabe was arrested? Would any of the townsfolk take his word that he was innocent? They hadn't in the past.

She put a hand to her head, suddenly needing to get away from these people who seemed so friendly, yet were so cruel to one of their own. "I have a headache. I think I'd like to go home."

Gabe slipped a finger under her chin and turned her face up to his. He gave her a puzzled frown. She lowered her lashes, unable to hold that probing gaze.

"All right," he said. He said good-night to the other couple. "Thanks for the invitation. We'll let you know."

Whitney realized she hadn't heard the invitation. She forced her attention to the matter at hand.

"Don't wait too long," Genny advised with a charming smile for both of them. "We'll be gone next weekend."

"Genny and I are getting married at her parents' home back east next Sunday," Rafe Barrett told them.

"Hmm," Gabe drawled.

Whitney could have kicked him for the mocking undertone. "Congratulations," she quickly filled in. "I'm sure you'll be very happy."

Rafe looked at his fiancée. "I have no doubt about that," he said in a quiet voice.

"Me, either," she agreed.

A heartbeat of silence ticked past.

"We'd better go," Gabe said. "The roads are supposed to ice over tonight. We'll see you." He guided Whitney to the coatroom and helped her change to her socks and boots. He seemed in a rush to leave now that she'd suggested it.

When he'd lifted her into the truck, he dashed around to the other side and cranked it up. Before they backed and turned toward the street, she saw the outline of a tall man as he, too, left the light and warmth inside the community center. He was wearing a black Stetson and pulled a thick coat on over his suit.

She watched behind them as they left, but didn't see a vehicle pull into the street. For some reason, she'd been sure the sheriff would follow them.

Facing forward again, she watched the glare of ice in the headlights for a while before she spoke. "Did you ever get a feeling something was happening, or going to happen, but you didn't know what it was?"

Gabe gave her a whip-flick of a glance, but said nothing.

"That's the way I feel," she said, watching him in the light of the dashboard as they picked up speed on the highway. "I can feel it coming closer... a premonition of danger... or something. I don't know..." She fell silent.

"I wouldn't have thought you'd be overtaken by a case of nerves," he drawled. "You'd better lay off those horror books you like to read."

He was lying to her. She felt it. His teasing tone was a cover for things he didn't want her to realize. She clamped her lips together and didn't say another word the rest of the way home.

Whitney stared at the shadows dancing across the tall ceiling. Her eyes were scratchy and dry. Her head ached. Endless thoughts ran in endless loops through her mind. She couldn't settle down to sleep.

Gabe's rough advice haunted her. He'd told her not to wear her heart on her sleeve and not to take premonitions seriously.

From now on, she'd be more careful. Her heart wouldn't be on display, nor would she share any more apprehensions with him. She'd watch and wait. Things were coming to a head. She could sense the swift approach of...events, fate, whatever.

She finally fell asleep. Shortly before dawn, she woke abruptly. A cold draft blew over her face. Pushing upright on an elbow, she pulled the shade back just enough to see out.

She watched as Gabe, dressed in dark clothing, moved like a shadow across the meadow by staying among the scattered trees and stands of shrub willow. He dipped under the top row of barbed wire and climbed through the fence, heading for the small grove of conifers near the boundary of their properties.

Another man met him there.

In the soft gray light, she saw Gabe glance toward the house, then motion the man back into the trees.

Whitney jumped out of bed and grabbed the binoculars from the mantel but was too late. The men had disappeared among the dark green branches of the trees.

Thirty minutes later she was about to give up when Gabe stepped out from behind a pine tree. He paused and surveyed the area, taking in the sweep of mountains to the north, the meadow and winding road leading to her house, and finally the house. He seemed to be staring at her window.

Although she knew he couldn't see her, she tensed, ready to run like a rabbit with a coyote in the vicinity. When he started across the meadow again, she rose and dressed. She was in the kitchen, the coffee brewing, when the front door opened and closed.

She heard the creak of the stairs, once as he went up, again when he came back down. The coffeepot gurgled a final time, then was quiet. She reached for two mugs and was pouring the coffee into them when he appeared at the kitchen door.

His dark glance took in her jeans, shirt and sweater. "You're up early," he commented.

"So are you." She set one mug on the table, then took a sip from the other.

"I had things to do." His tone challenged her to make something of it. He watched her like a cat, steady and unblinking.

"Such as?" She sensed he was angry, but wasn't sure of the cause—the man in the woods or the fact that she'd seen them.

To her surprise, a smile appeared, curling up the corners of his mouth. "Dauntless to the end," he muttered.

"You aren't going to tell me," she concluded.

He took a drink of coffee, then set the mug down. "No, I'm not going to tell you. You said you trusted me. Prove it."

"How?" she asked warily.

"Don't ask any more questions. Don't worry about what I'm doing or what's going to happen. It's not your problem, and I don't want to have to worry about you as well as...other things."

He was asking for blind faith. She swallowed hard. "I can't help worrying, but I won't interfere." Unless he needed her again.

His dark gaze probed relentlessly into her soul.

"I promise," she said. And wondered if she'd keep it.

Chapter Eight

Whitney stopped in the middle of the living room and surveyed the furniture she and Gabe had brought up from the basement and down from the attic. "No, I don't like that."

He gave a snort.

She ignored him. "Let's move the sideboard over there—"

"That's where it was two moves ago," he observed, making a great show of resigned patience.

"Yes, it's definitely the right place. Grab that end." She lifted her end of the solid walnut sideboard and shuffled along backward when he lifted the other end.

They eased it into place on the north side of the living room. Whitney fell back against the newly papered wall, her breath coming in labored pants.

"Take a break," Gabe advised.

"No, I want to get the rest of the stuff in place. Let's put the butler's table and those chairs in front of the west windows. Can you believe anyone would paint curly maple? I'll strip it when I get the upstairs done."

With Gabe's help, she arranged the furniture she'd decided to use in the living room and antechamber. When they finished the task, he leaned against the wall with his thumbs hooked into his back pockets while she turned around in a circle and examined the room with a critical eye.

"Yes," she said. "It's perfect. Or will be when the rest of the furniture is refinished. The sideboard looks wonderful."

She had stripped off the chipped and stained varnish, sanded it until the wood was satin smooth, stained it, then coated it with wood sealer. Now it glowed with a soft patina, ready for the buffet meals she intended to serve from it.

The tiny, old-fashioned stove was in place, all cleaned and polished. The coffee and teapots would go there.

The drapes had been cleaned and hung. Sheer gold curtains under them softened the outside glare. Two camelback sofas and two chairs had been upholstered in golden brown velveteen. They formed a conversation square in the middle of the room. The wallpaper was pale gold with a thin apricot stripe.

She glanced at the Norman Rockwell calendar on the wall behind the office counter, which Gabe had made from the leftover closet panels. February first. She might be open for business by the first of March if the plumbers finished in time.

The sewing room was being converted to a bathroom. That would make two full-size baths upstairs. Each bedroom was to have its own half bath. These would be installed in the tiny closets, a rather close fit, but it would do. Armoires and chiffoniers would replace the closets.

"I'd like to hold an open house by the end of the month, sort of introduce the place to the local businesspeople. Do you think we can be ready?"

"Maybe."

"I saw some clothes in the trunks in the attic. I'm going to look for a dress when I finish papering the upstairs hall. Maybe I can find something suitably Victorian to wear for the opening. What are you going to do this afternoon?"

"I'll work on the windows." He'd been recaulking windows for the past week. He was also keeping an eye on the plumbers.

She nodded and headed for the stairs. The telephone rang. She changed course, going to the office under the steps, and lifted the receiver. "B&B Inn," she said, liking the official way the simple name sounded.

A man wanted to know if she had two rooms available for the weekend. He said the resort had recommended her place.

"This weekend?" she said. "I'm sorry, but I won't be op—"

The phone was taken out of her hand. "This is the reservation desk. I'll check our calendar," Gabe said smoothly.

He gave Whitney a mocking grin when she glared at him.

"Um, we won't have any rooms available before March, I'm afraid. I have an opening the weekend of the fourth." He named a price that was much more than she'd planned on charging.

She waited until he wrote down a name, address and phone number, and hung up. "That was terrible, to lie to that man about the rooms—"

"Did I lie?" Gabe challenged.

"You told him we were booked up."

"No, I said we wouldn't have rooms available until March. That's true, isn't it?"

"Well, yes... but you implied—"

"What he thought was his business," Gabe cut her off. "If you're going to make a success of this place, you better play it a little closer to the chest. Where would you rather stay—an inn that's obviously frequented by others or one that's so new no one knows anything about it?"

Put like that, she tried to decide how she'd react. "I'd have to look at them," she said defensively.

"Exactly. If you can't do that, you choose the one that seems the most popular." He handed her the note, then headed for the basement for his tools.

"The rate you quoted was too high," she continued her argument to his back. "Families can't afford that much per room."

He swung around. "Go for the yuppie crowd," he advised. "They can afford to travel. You should take out ads in those glossy travel magazines you see in doctors' offices. That's where the money is. Emphasize the healthy aspects of the place—the great outdoors, no pollution, hiking, riding, tuning in on nature, that sort of thing."

"I was thinking more middle of the road," she explained. "A sort of homey place for families with kids, people who can't afford the prices at the resort, but who would love to come here."

He studied her for a long minute, then smiled, reluctantly, she thought.

"Yeah, that sounds like you." With a shake of his head, he went down the steps to the basement.

Whitney savored that wry, almost tender smile for a second. Then she entered the information from the note in the appointment schedule. Her first guests, she realized. It seemed momentous. She swallowed to dislodge the lump in her throat. She was truly in business, it seemed.

When she found time late that afternoon, she went up to the attic. It looked bare. She'd thrown a lot of stuff away.

All the furniture had been moved into the rooms where she planned to use it. There were only a few boxes and trunks left to be looked through. She opened a large steamer trunk.

In it, she found a wedding dress.

She scarcely breathed as she lifted the silk confection of satin and lace from the muslin wrapping. Her grandmother's wedding outfit. She recognized it from a picture. A veil and gloves of the sheerest lace fell to the floor. She picked them up.

The veil was attached to a ribbon sewn with delicate embroidered forget-me-nots. She released her braid from the top of her head and let it fall down her back. She tied the ribbon around her head and settled the silk around her shoulders. It made a whispering sound as it fell into place.

Going to one of the windows set in a gable, she peered at her reflection. She tried to smile, but couldn't. The moment seemed too solemn. Instead she thought of all the hopes and dreams the outfit symbolized.

On impulse, she slipped out of her shoes, shirt and jeans, then stepped into the dress. It had probably touched the floor when her grandmother had worn it, but on her, it was ballerina length.

She held the row of tiny satin-covered buttons and hand-stitched buttonholes together in the back. Yes, it would close.

A darkly compelling male face appeared beside hers in the glass pane. Without a word, Gabe began fastening the buttons down her back. Her heart seemed to shake her entire body with each beat.

Her skin burned when his fingers lightly brushed her as he moved down the row. She was aware of the material tightening over her breasts and down her rib cage as he slipped each button into place. Three inches below her breasts, the satin flared into a gored skirt, simple in its lines, timeless in its beauty.

When he finished, he moved to her hair. With supple skill, he unfastened her braid and combed his fingers through it until her hair hung in shimmering waves down her back.

She turned toward him, a marionette directed by invisible strings. Fires blazed in the depths of his eyes, engulfing her in his masculine desires. She knew she would go to him if he asked, and never count the cost.

The moment stretched into forever.

"A bride should look happy, not apprehensive," he said.

"I'm not a bride."

He reached out and found the edge of the veil. Slowly he drew it up until it cleared her face, then he let it fall behind her head.

She licked her lips, parting them so she was ready for his kiss. She wanted him with a desperation that was filled with all the longing she'd experienced since knowing him. He was her true mate, and she wanted the full mating ritual...all of it.

"Please," she murmured.

"I haven't time for this. It's...wrong, not part of the plan." He sounded weary and exasperated with life.

"Why? How can it be wrong when we both want it?" Only this moment made sense to her. She reached for him.

He caught her wrists and wouldn't let her touch him. "I have nothing to give you," he told her.

"Yourself."

"That's not enough. You have to live here. Do you want a name that brings suspicion to the eye whenever someone hears it?"

"I don't care."

"People never forget. The whispers will always circulate. Like that day I went to town with you. Like at the dance the other night. I saw the wariness in the people who remembered my name. I knew what they were thinking." His voice dropped to a whisper as he repeated the local gossip.

"'There's the Deveraux boy...the one who was a thief.' Do you want that following you all your life?"

Whitney's heart ached for him. "They'd see you differently if you lived here and proved them wrong."

"By living an exemplary life? Human nature doesn't work like that, Irish. Before long, I'd start to resent it, then I wouldn't give a damn what they thought... and it would show. I'd grow to hate it here, just like I did before."

"It would be different this time. I'd be with you."

He closed his eyes for a second, then sighed and studied her anxious gaze. "You almost make a believer out of me. Almost," he added when she would have leapt upon this statement.

She blinked rapidly, but the tears insisted on forming.

He released her wrists and lifted one hand to her face. He brushed away the two drops that clung to her lower lashes and rubbed the moisture between his fingers as if he'd never seen tears and wasn't sure what they were.

"Ah, God, Irish," he said as he pulled her into his arms.

For a second she saw his eyes—haunted eyes, filled with longing, with anguish. Then his lips were wild on hers, the kiss so sweet, it stole her breath and made her legs weak.

She wanted him to come to her, not only in passion, but with joy and faith in the future. She turned her head. He followed the line of her cheek to her neck and nibbled there.

"Gabe," she said, wanting to discuss this important point, but she sounded breathless. She wasn't going to be able to say no. The word wasn't in her where he was concerned.

"Yes?" He kissed along her collarbone. His long, slender fingers touched her waist, then glided upward. He moved in close.

Her hips were pressed to the windowsill. She twisted from side to side, trying to deny the passion... except it kept getting mixed up with the love she felt for this man... this rogue who refused to trust anyone very deeply...this dark intruder into her sunny plans...

Her feeble struggle produced an instant response in him.

"Be still," he said, his voice deep and husky.

She froze in place. The seductive sound of his breathing rasped near her ear. She felt the hair stirring at her temple with each exhalation.

The warmth of his hands penetrated the bodice of the satin gown, resting just below her breasts. She ached to have him touch her there.

He lifted his head and stared into her eyes. "Going once," he said. "Going twice..."

"What?" she asked, hardly aware of what she said. All her senses were attuned to the wonderfully masculine feel of him plastered along the length of her.

"Drowning," he murmured, "going down for the third time."

She knew the feeling. "I...yes...me, too." She lifted her mouth to his and caught his lower lip between her teeth. Holding him captive, she leaned into his strength.

A shudder went through him and into her. He gave her his mouth and let her do whatever she wanted. She'd never been so free to taste and caress, to experiment and explore.

Suddenly he took the lead again. His tongue probed for entry. His body demanded response. She opened her lips to him.

When his foot touched hers, she moved her leg so that he could slide his muscular thigh between hers.

"Never," she half moaned as he kissed all over her face. "I've never felt this way."

"I know," he soothed and aroused at the same time. "It's so damned strong. Powerful."

"Yes."

"Open a bit more. Yes, like that. Kiss me hard...harder."

She tried to give him everything he wanted from her. And a little bit more... the little bit that was her heart.

When he cupped her breast, she couldn't suppress the almost silent cry of pleasure that rushed through her. At the back of her neck, his fingers found the tiny buttons he'd fastened. He opened them... one by one by one. Then he slipped the material off her shoulders and down her arms. It pooled around her waist.

"I want to see you," he told her. "I've never seen you."

She could hardly breathe when he reached behind her. He unfastened the hooks, and her bra slid from her.

His eyes seared her with the heat of his gaze. "I knew you'd be beautiful." He traced a path down her throat, following the vee of lightly tanned skin down her chest. "The freckles stop."

"They... they only appear where I get the sun."

"If it were up to me, you'd never wear anything." He brushed his fingertips over one breast, then the other, so very gently.

That sounded so impossibly romantic to her—a modern day Adam and Eve in their own private garden of delight. "I'd like that," she exclaimed, desperate for that paradise. "To be free to roam the fields...to make love wherever and whenever we wanted."

"By the creek. There's a shady spot in summer, under a willow, with moss growing over the ground. I'd make love to you there." He bent and kissed the very tip of each breast.

Spirals of feeling jolted down inside her. She was caught up in the wonder of it. She closed her eyes. "Oh, yes."

"And in the mountains. There are places there..." He kissed her eyes, her nose, her lips...soft, soft touches. "There are places..."

"So wonderful," she breathed, nearly weeping in her need to go to those places with him. "It would be wonderful."

"Yes," he agreed. "You tremble when I touch you, and it nearly kills me to let you go."

She heard the note of regret and opened her eyes, alarmed by it. He watched her, the fire in his eyes darkening to embers, as if it had blazed so high it had burned itself out.

He stroked her cheek. "It would be heaven and hell and everything in between. Every part of you is like a promise of all the good things to come. If we were to make love..."

She realized the moment had passed, that they weren't going to make love at all. The disappointment was a keen-edged cry deep inside, shattering her dreams of a moment ago.

"Why can't we?" she demanded. She grasped the sweatshirt he wore, handfuls of cotton, as if she could hold him by force.

"I have things I have to do." The darkness returned to his eyes. "Then..."

She waited for him to complete the thought, but he didn't. Then what? she wanted to demand. In her heart she feared he would never trust her enough to risk his own heart.

He stepped back. He ran his gaze over her once more, but it was as if he were looking at a painting he knew he'd never see again. He wanted to carry the memory with him when he left.

"The bathroom is finished," he said. "That's what I came up to tell you. You can check it out and let the plumber know if it's okay tomorrow." He headed for the stairs.

She listened to the sound of his retreating footsteps. When she could no longer hear them, she unfastened the rest of the buttons and put on her clothes. The Cinderella interlude was over. It was back to the cold, cruel world.

After storing the wedding gown, she sorted through the rest of the boxes, keeping some things, tossing others. It was dark by the time she finished. When she went downstairs, reluctant to face Gabe, she found she needn't have worried.

He was gone.

Whitney paced the floor, resentful of every second that ticked by on the clock. It was after midnight, and Gabe was still out.

She tried to remember the promise she'd made—that she wouldn't interfere in his affairs. She clenched her fists and paced to the window. She almost wished he were having an affair. Then she'd at least know he was safe inside for the night.

Her heart shied at the thought of him in the arms and bed of another woman. She wanted him safe with her, in her arms, in her bed, sharing warmth and happiness.

Stalking to the window, she pulled the shade back a fraction of an inch and stared into the dark.

The new moon lighted the patches of snow in the meadow to a pale gloss. The truck was a black shadow beside the house. Gabe had no transportation that she knew of.

She peered at the barely discernible ranch buildings in the distance. He had to be at his ranch. At this moment he might be confronting the thieves, furious that they were using his property and putting the final blemish on his reputation.

No, he wouldn't do anything so foolish. He was wary, savvy to the dangers of the world. But he was also angry and hurt.

Trust me.

His words echoed in her mind. She'd given her word not to interfere. But if he were lying hurt and bleeding in the snow... if he'd been shot and left for dead...

God help her, but she didn't know what to do. She could call the sheriff and demand that he check out the Deveraux ranch. Gabe would be furious if she did and he was all right.

Trust me.

But if he needed help . . .

She paced again. Stopping in front of the fireplace, she stared at the embers left from the fire. Sighing, she added another log and settled in the chair with the afghan over her. She would wait another hour, then she was going to do something. She didn't know what.

Whitney woke with a jerk. "Oh-h," she groaned, and rubbed her stiff neck. She realized she was in the chair. Her gaze went to her empty bed as she remembered waiting up for Gabe.

She freshened up, put her hair back with a clip, then went into the silent kitchen. Six o'clock and no one there.

Gabe was always up before her, the coffee ready when she came in. Sometimes he had the meal prepared, too.

She cooked oatmeal and sausage, then made a huge platter of toast. Breakfast was ready. Swallowing the lump in her throat, she went up the steps. His door was closed, as usual.

After knocking twice, she took a breath and opened the door. The bed was empty, its covers neatly made. She couldn't tell if it had been used during the night.

On the dresser stood a small bowl that held some loose change. That was the only sign of occupancy in the room. No clothes on the floor or draped over the end of the bed. No brush, comb, or personal items visible. It gave her an eerie feeling, as if he'd never existed at all.

She opened the closet door. His suitcase and duffel bag were there, his clothing inside. He could leave in a minute if he so desired or needed to for some reason.

Her worry increasing tenfold, she closed the closet door and left the room. She ate breakfast at the white wrought-iron table. The gold-and-pink striped cushions of the matching chairs mocked her with their false cheer.

He could be lying in the snow, hurt and unconscious, just as he'd been the other time, she fretted. She ate the last bite of oatmeal. He could be bleeding to death. She choked down a piece of toast. He might be calling her name, needing her to come to him. She stood abruptly.

Going to the closet in her room, she yanked a sweater over her shirt, then pulled on her parka. She tucked her hair under a black knitted hat and jerked on insulated boots over heavy socks.

Grabbing her warmest gloves, she headed down the hall and out the door. A sense of déjà vu haunted her, but this time there wasn't a dark lump in the snow to be investigated. This time she'd have to rely on instinct alone to find him.

Going from tree to bush to tree, she slipped across the meadow. The ground was visible in most places, becoming mushy under her feet as the sun melted the snow more each day. She crossed the barbed-wire fence and dashed into the evergreens.

She paused in the shadows to catch her breath and let her heart slow down. She had to be calm and able to think clearly in case there was a problem. If she saw anything the slightest bit suspicious, she decided she'd head for home and call the sheriff.

With that in mind, she slinked through the small grove until another stand of pines was between her and the ranch house.

She dashed from one cover to another until she made her way behind the closest building, a small, ramshackle shed. Peering through a crack, she saw nesting boxes. A chicken house.

No one seemed to be around.

The silence was hard on the nerves. She listened intently, but heard only the low moan of the wind. Gathering her courage, she eased around the corner and slipped behind a barn.

The barn door sagged on its rusty hinges, leaving a six-inch gap between it and the frame. She squeezed inside.

Her heart stopped at the sight that greeted her. Crates of office equipment were stacked and covered with clear plastic—computers, laser printers, copiers, fax machines—half a million dollars' worth, she estimated.

For just a second her faith in Gabe wavered at the evidence before her eyes. Her heart insisted on believing in him, but what if it was wrong?

No. She wouldn't think that. She'd looked into his eyes and seen his soul. He was *not* part of the gang. He was here to clear his name.

So why couldn't he tell her that? Was it asking too much that he confide in her? She shook her head against the doubts.

She started to wind her way around the loot when she froze. A noise. Over her head. She looked toward the loft and stared into eyes staring back at her.

Every muscle in her body jerked.

The owl blinked once, then fixed its gaze on her again. Whitney pressed a hand over her pounding heart. Hardly daring to breathe, she made her way to the front of the barn and pressed her face to a crack.

She could see the old ranch house, its windows broken, most of the roof caved in. The garage door was open. No vehicles were inside. She sighed in relief. No one was there.

Not at the present, she corrected with a glance at the stolen goods stacked behind her. She made a circuit of the barn, but found no evidence of Gabe or signs of a struggle.

Feeling somewhat bolder, she searched the other buildings. Nothing. It had probably been a foolish notion to come over there, anyway. She'd sneak back home and get to work before Gabe showed up.

If he did.

No, she wasn't going to think like that. Nothing was wrong. He wasn't a thief. He wasn't in trouble. He was a grown man, fully capable of taking care of himself.

Unless he'd been caught and was outnumbered.

She could drive herself crazy trying to figure it out. She had to make a decision . . . an important decision.

If he wasn't at the house when she arrived, she was going to call the sheriff and report the stolen goods.

Or maybe she should call Gabe's friend, the resort owner. She could casually ask if Gabe was there.

If Gabe was at the house, she would...she would ask him if he knew about the stolen equipment. She'd ask . . . she couldn't. He'd know she hadn't kept her promise if she said anything.

She closed her eyes in despair. She didn't know what to do.

Gabe stood among the weeds of the little cemetery and stared at the distant vista. The hill gave him a good view of the land around him, including the ranch and Whitney's property.

A cloud lurked on the horizon. Another blizzard was predicted. That fact might make the thieves decide to move their loot before the roads were closed again.

God, he hoped so. He was tired of waiting. He wanted to get on with his life. Get on to . . . where?

He sighed and sat down on a tombstone. A picture of a blue-eyed, redheaded woman came to him. Whitney. He didn't know what to do about her.

I'm a stayin' kind of woman. You're a leavin' kind of man.

That song summed the situation up. He'd tried to warn her. When he left, he didn't want any hard feelings between them.

When he left . . .

He struck his thigh with the flat of his hand, angry with life. He'd had his plans mapped out—catch the crooks, sell the ranch, leave. As simple as one, two, three.

Except a redheaded harridan had thrown him for a loop. His head was still spinning from the impact. She thought he could have a life on the ranch, that the locals would forget the past and accept him as he was now.

He knew better. At the first hint of trouble, he'd be a suspect. He'd learned that long ago. All his memories of the ranch and the town were unhappy ones.

On his mental screen, Whitney gave him a scolding frown. All right, so he had some new memories that weren't so bad. So what?

Like a movie, the past month flashed on his inner vision—working with Whitney, laughing with her at their comical faces covered in plaster dust except where the mask had covered their noses, seeing her in the attic in the old wedding dress...kissing her...wanting her...

Crazy. The whole thing with her was crazy. She wasn't part of his plans. And yet...

Sometimes, when he looked at her, he thought of home and family, of friendship that lasted longer than the job at hand. Another vision came to him—the one in which he was running across a meadow, laughing and holding hands with a redheaded female, but this time the female wasn't Whitney. It was a little girl with trusting blue eyes and freckles on her nose. Her hair was dark, like his. His daughter...

He stood abruptly and headed for the exit. No use dreaming of what couldn't be. A man who didn't learn from his past mistakes was stupid. Period.

A furtive movement in the meadow below caused him to pause after he closed the gate to the cemetery. He went into full alert.

After a moment he detected movement again. A shadow slipped through the grove of evergreen trees. When it stopped, it blended with the trees. If he hadn't been looking, he wouldn't have known someone was there.

He put his hand in his pocket and eased the safety off the automatic. A beat of excitement went through him. It looked like something was about to happen. He schooled himself to the cold, calculating patience he'd learned long ago.

When the shadowy figure was far enough along for him to be sure where the person was going, he began to follow. Maintaining his position of advantage above the other man, he slipped silently through the trees that circled the graveyard and hurried down to the creek that divided the two properties.

Yeah, the guy was heading for the B&B.

Gabe speeded up. He'd seen one of the thieves hanging around the ranch earlier. It was the first time a watch had been posted with the stolen goods. That could indicate the loot was going to be moved soon. For now, though, he had to figure out why someone was heading toward Whitney's place.

If the crooks had heard he was in town and working for her, if one of them knew who he was... Hmm, maybe someone was supposed to keep on eye on him to make sure he didn't interrupt their plans.

That could be another indication things were coming to a head. Good. It couldn't be too soon for him. Then he'd shake the dust off his heels and get out of there.

For a second he thought of the blue-eyed, redheaded woman who was probably pacing the floor right now at the house and wondering where he was. Fate hadn't been kind when it had thrown Whitney at him, teasing him with her lips, her smiles, her dreams. He'd miss her, he admitted. He'd miss her...

He had to concentrate and not miss his footing when the field became rough with a stone outcropping, plus keep a low profile in case the thief was watching for intruders.

Once down the slope, he broke into a ground-eating jog. He was out of sight of the other person. Of course, that meant the man was out of his sight, too, but this was the logical place to cross the barbed-wire fence after jumping the narrow creek a bit further up.

Slipping between two boulders, he pulled the gun from his pocket and waited. He wanted to see who the bastard was. He had a gut feeling he'd know the man.

It was probably one of the local citizens. Maybe someone he'd gone to school with.

He shook his head slightly, not letting his eyes waver from the fence and the woods beyond them. It had been too long since he'd lived there. All his school chums had surely drifted to other parts of the world long ago, just as he had.

Sixteen years. A lot of drifting in that time. He was getting tired. And old, he mocked himself. It was time he was getting out of the covert intelligence business.

He thought of Whitney and the strange longings she stirred in him. No time for that, not now, maybe not ever.

She said she trusted him. Maybe she did. But what if the time came when it was his word against someone else's? Would she side with him when it came down to the crunch? He doubted it. No one else had, not his father, his high school principal, not the pastor at church or the sheriff at that time.

He stared at the woods grimly. Where the hell was the man he'd been tracking? Maybe he'd outguessed himself.

A shadow loomed among the firs and pines beyond the fence. Gabe positioned the gun. If he had to shoot, he'd aim for the shoulder. That was a nice incapacitating wound; then he had a few questions he wanted answered.

The shadow slinked out of the trees, bending low, heading for the barbed wire. Gabe cursed silently.

He watched Whitney make her furtive way to the house. She'd been over to the ranch, spying on him.

So much for trust.

Chapter Nine

Whitney bent and slipped between the strands, careful not to catch her parka on the sharp barbs. She felt like a fool. Now she had to get back to the house before Gabe showed up and found out she'd broken her promise not to interfere.

Well, she'd been worried. That was natural.

However, she'd decided that he had gotten up earlier than usual and gone fishing or skiing or hiking. Whatever. She'd go home and get to work. She'd be very nonchalant when he showed up. She wouldn't ask him where he'd been or anything like that. She wouldn't pry.

She wouldn't let him know of that one moment of distrust that had flitted through her.

Upon reaching the house, she crept inside. No one was there. She felt the emptiness and swallowed against a sudden tightness in her throat. He might never come back—

She heard the crunch of gravel outside, then a tall, masculine figure appeared on the steps. She opened the door and faced Gabe.

"Where have you been all night?" she demanded, suddenly furious with him for all her needless worrying. She clamped her lips together, but it was too late to call back the accusing words.

"Were you checking on me?" he asked in a soft tone that made her want to run for cover.

She thought of the anxious hours she'd spent, the uneasy sleep in the chair, the quick, nervous check of his room. She thought of the stolen goods stacked in his barn.

"Of course not." She felt the flush rise in her face.

He saw right through the lie. "I saw you coming from the ranch. You promised you wouldn't interfere. You gave your word."

When he moved a step closer, she moved a step back. Guilt for breaking her promise gnawed at her, but it was overpowered by other factors. Her heart told her he had nothing to do with the theft. But what if she were wrong?

She'd seen the evidence with her own eyes. His ranch was being used for illegal purposes. Surely an innocent person would have called the sheriff.

Unless he thought he could capture them single-handedly? Men could be such dolts about things like asking for help....

The tension increased as the silence lengthened. Please trust me, she wanted to plea. Explain what you're doing. Trust me with your secrets.

As she trusted him?

Looking into his eyes, her doubts fled. Maybe she was being a fool, but she saw goodness and honor in him. While she studied him, his expression changed, becoming hard and withdrawn. For a second she worried that he'd seen her misgivings, but how could he identify what she refused to fully acknowledge herself?

"Were you there?" she finally asked.

"Does it matter? Haven't you already decided my guilt or innocence?" he demanded.

She looked away from his probing glance, unable to admit the doubts that had bothered her.

"Stay out of my life," he said with great finality, as if he'd seen into the very depths of her soul and been disappointed. "As long as I do the work you've hired me to do, my time is my own. What I choose to do with the rest of it is my concern, not yours. Understand?"

It was hard to believe this harsh stranger was the same man who had kissed her so very gently and passionately less than twenty-four hours ago. But he was.

He was also a man who'd been alone too long. He'd never share anything with her, not his thoughts or feelings, not even passion.

"Yes," she said, "I understand." She lifted her chin. "What should I do with your clothes if you disappear like you did last night and fail to return?"

The question, and perhaps the cool control she displayed, surprised him. He hesitated, then said, "Give them to the Salvation Army."

She nodded. Turning, she headed for her room. She felt infinitely weary. The inner light that had always guided her seemed to have dimmed.

That admission troubled her. The dream she'd labored over for so long no longer held first place in her life, but there was nothing to fill the void. She was afraid there never would be.

At the door, she glanced back over her shoulder.

Gabe still stood there in the hall. He was gazing across the room and out the window. His eyes were narrowed against the glare, and the attractive crinkles appeared at the corners. As she'd first thought, they weren't laugh lines, but those of a man used to gazing into the far distance.

She wondered what he saw in the vastness of the winter landscape. Did the snow-covered mountains call to his soul? Did the river urge him to seek other horizons and not stay in one place too long?

He'd lived at her house for more than a month, but she was no closer to his heart. He didn't give any part of himself away. He refused her attempts to defend him or to aid in his mission. He didn't want anything from her.

Rogue. Maverick. Loner.

All the names fit. They all excluded her.

She went into her room and removed her outdoor clothing. There was work to be done. By the end of the month, she had to have the B&B Inn ready for those important first guests. From now on, she would keep her mind on her business and not on the urgings of her heart.

Whitney smoothed the last piece of wallpaper on the wall of the guest bedroom. She closed the bucket of paste and headed for the bathroom to wash out the brush.

The scent of homemade soup drifting up the stairs reminded her that she hadn't had lunch yet. She'd put on a big pot to simmer after breakfast that morning. It was now almost two o'clock.

Gabe was working upstairs. They hadn't spoken more than ten words since the scene between them two days ago.

She went to the kitchen and spooned up two bowls. After setting them on the table to cool, she toasted whole wheat bagels and put them on a plate along with a stack of crackers. She set her lips grimly and walked up the steps to the room where he was painting the chair rail and windowsills.

Pausing on the threshold, she watched him for a couple of minutes. "I've never known anyone who needed binoculars to paint a windowsill," she said with acerbic nonchalance.

He whipped around, smudging paint on the window from the brush he held in one hand. In the other, he held her binoculars.

After muttering a curse, he set the field glasses on a small table pushed into the center of the room and wiped the glass clean. He dropped the brush into a jar of water and fastened the lid on the paint can. "I was watching some ducks on the creek. The painting is finished."

Things were drawing to a close. She sensed it. "Good," she said. "Lunch is ready."

She was pleased with her composure. He wouldn't have cause to accuse her of wearing her heart on her sleeve nor of interfering in his life ever again. She marched back down the steps and took her seat at the tiny table.

He followed after washing up. They ate in silence.

"That was good," he said when he finished.

"Thank you."

Gabe noticed she didn't meet his eyes, not once during the meal, or at any time during the past two days. It didn't matter. He was pretty sure she'd seen the equipment at the ranch. And suspected him of vile deeds. He'd seen the doubts in her eyes when he'd stepped up on the porch and she'd opened the door.

He forced the bitterness of that instant from his mind. Hell, what had he expected? That she'd take his side on blind faith?

Why didn't he tell her the truth? The job would be over soon. The sheriff had contacted him. The goods would be moved within the next twenty-four hours according to their informant. The net was drawing tight and all would be over soon. Then everyone, including Irish, would know the truth.

For some reason that didn't bring him a great deal of satisfaction. He'd looked forward to grinding the locals' noses in the truth, but it no longer carried the savage pleasure of triumph that he'd once anticipated.

He stared grimly at the steam rising from the pot on the stove. Irish and her "homey" atmosphere, he scoffed. He'd be glad to get the hell away from there. He'd get back to his job—maybe stop and see his old business partner, Riley Houston, and his wife, back in West Virginia first—then head for far horizons. There was a whole world out there...

The thought died.

His life seemed empty, his goals paltry. A vulnerability he never felt before assailed him.

Damn Whitney and what she did to him! He had to get out of the house. He'd go to town, see the sheriff, eat dinner out. That should occupy a few hours. He carried his dishes to the sink, rinsed them and put them in the dishwasher.

"Look," he said, "I'm sorry for any trouble I've brought to you. I didn't plan on meeting you...on the attraction..." He waved his hand in a futile gesture.

Whitney realized he felt sorry for her. Pity was the one thing she wouldn't accept. "It doesn't matter," she said.

"Doesn't it?" He smiled briefly, bitterly. "Life has a way of tripping people up and shattering all our good intentions. I wish...things could be different."

"I'm okay," she insisted, clinging stubbornly to her pride. "An attraction is not a lifetime devotion."

With that, she rose and left the kitchen. In her room, she paced restlessly. Finally, feeling she had to get away, she decided to go to town. She would shop, take in a movie, anything to get out of the house for a few hours.

She showered and dressed in blue wool slacks. She chose a sweater in red, white and blue stripes. A ribbon barrette held her hair at the base of her neck. She put on makeup and added earrings of red, white and blue beads to match her top. There, she mocked, that perked her spirits right up.

Grabbing her parka and gloves, she headed for the door. Gabe came down the stairs at the same moment. They looked at each other in wary surprise.

"I was going to ask to use the truck," he said, "but I can see you're going out."

His eyes raked her outfit. A light seemed to flare in them for a second, then he blinked, and it was gone. She decided it had been her imagination.

He wore dark brown cords with a white shirt and brown suede jacket. His dark hair gleamed under the polished crystal of the chandelier she'd cleaned with such high expectations a week ago. He pushed a wave off his forehead.

"I'm going to Ashland," she told him. She didn't ask him to join her. The purpose of the trip was to be alone.

He nodded. "I could use a haircut."

She frowned in discouragement. She couldn't admit his presence disturbed her. "I'm going to do some shopping. I might not be back for several hours."

"I have a couple of things to do there, too," he said. He gave her a look that said he could be as stubborn as she.

His smile disclosed nothing, but it disarmed her nonetheless. He was a handsome daredevil of a man, a man used to taking risks. She stared into his eyes, trying to decipher his mood.

There was an air of recklessness about him tonight, she decided. It undermined her defenses.

"I may go to a play," she warned, trying to dissuade him from the trip one more time.

"Hmm," was all he said.

She couldn't tell if that was agreement or not. Giving up, she dug the keys out of her purse. He opened the door, closed it behind them and waited until she locked it before going to the truck. There, he gallantly held the truck door for her, too.

She wondered what kind of game he was playing. If he was trying to confuse her, he was succeeding, she thought irritably.

When he was inside, she started the truck and drove off, her mind mulling over the evening ahead. Since the trip took an hour, she had lots of time to speculate. She was no nearer to guessing his motives when they arrived in town than she'd been at the start of the journey...or from their first meeting, truth be told.

She sighed, discouraged with life.

She drove to a block of small boutiques and found a parking place. "What time shall we meet?" she asked. "And where?"

He checked his watch, one of those with several functions that pilots and divers wear. "Here at the truck? Two hours?"

"All right." She climbed out and walked into the first shop, aware of his eyes on her. After she was inside, she glanced out the window. He was nowhere in sight.

He had the ability to silently appear and disappear like a cat. She recalled the day she'd found him, how he had looked all around upon regaining consciousness, his gaze swiftly assessing the situation, his senses always alert. There were other instances where he'd reacted in ways that only someone used to living in danger would react.

She tried to imagine the life of a sixteen-year-old, out in the world, on his own, with no one to give a damn about him and no one for him to trust. He had survived, but what price had he paid in his soul for that survival?

Again, the sense of time running out came to her and with it, a sense of sadness. Putting the useless thoughts aside, she searched through the racks until she found a long black skirt with a wide sash of shocking pink. With a white blouse and her cameo of pink onyx, it would do for a hostess outfit. She tried the skirt on and decided to buy it.

She went to four other places before she found the blouse she wanted. It was white and made of silk organza. The sleeves were full and pleated. The neckline dipped into a low vee edged with lace. Perfect. She looked at the price and did a quick mental calculation. "I'll take it."

Allowing herself only a fleeting worry about the cost—after all, she had to have the proper clothing for her business—she put it on her credit card for next month's bills.

Glancing at the time as she left the store, she saw she was ten minutes late. Gabe waited by the truck. He didn't take his eyes off her while she approached him.

"Ready?" he asked. Taking the keys, he put her bags inside the truck, then he hesitated. "How about dinner?"

She gave him a startled glance. Food had been far from her thoughts, but she realized it had been hours since their last meal.

Her mouth suddenly dry, she nodded. Silly, she scolded. This was simply dinner. They'd eaten together every night for five weeks. Being in a restaurant was no big thing.

He took her arm and escorted her across the street and down the sidewalk to a little place tucked between two taller buildings. Her skin glowed where his hand rested lightly.

The light was appropriately dim inside the restaurant. Gabe asked for a table for two.

Whitney shot Gabe a troubled glance. A table for two sounded terribly intimate. He returned her look without comment. There was anger in him, but she recognized it as the anger of longing and denial, of wanting and not having.

The blood pounded thickly through her body. The night held a thousand possibilities. She wanted him, too, and she saw no reason to deny it at all.

By the time they were seated at an intimate booth surrounded by plants and bronze Plexiglas panels, they could have been on another planet for all she knew. She let her eyes feast on him.

He looked different with the fresh haircut...more the ruthless tycoon than the wild, primitive man she'd imagined when she'd first seen him. But he was still her love...her special love.

"Your eyes give you away," he said. Even shaded with anger, his tone was more of a caress than a reprimand.

She made a show of unfolding her napkin and laying it in her lap to hide the flutter of her nerves. When she glanced up, her eyes locked with his.

Secret messages, so fleeting she couldn't read them, flew between them. Tonight was different. She knew it.

Yes.

He looked at her with tenderness.

Yes.

She looked into his eyes and saw his soul.

Yes.

"I'll take you right here if you keep looking at me like that," he warned.

"It's how you're looking at me," she retorted, feeling deliciously feminine and alluring.

"I know," he murmured wryly. "But one of us is supposed to be sensible."

Warmth exploded outward from some dark, primal place where only passion and emotion dwelled. She felt dizzy, faint with longing. "Why?" she challenged softly.

"Do you need a few more minutes?" a polite voice intervened.

Whitney looked at the menu. She didn't need any more time at all. Neither did Gabe. *Tonight*. Her heart shook her with its wild beating.

"Shall we splurge?" he asked, quiet resignation rippling through his voice like the silvery murmuring of a mountain brook. "The steak and lobster?"

She nodded. What did food matter?

He ordered for them, then the waitress went away and they were alone again, as much as a couple could be when surrounded by twenty other couples. She smiled tentatively, afraid to trust this strange intimacy, unable not to.

Their privacy enclosed them like a golden bubble, isolating them in their own private garden. Her heart ached with the wonder of it all. Love was the most precarious of emotions.

When their salads arrived, along with wine and a hot loaf of fresh bread, Gabe sliced a piece and buttered it before giving it to her. When he held it out—almost like a love offering—she took it with trembling fingers.

"You affect me, too." His confession shocked her.

She tried to figure out where this...this delicate love play was going. The distance between them was gone, the rules he'd forced upon them subtly altered. She couldn't figure out why.

Don't think, she told her logical self. Just take whatever the moment offers and don't count the cost.

She wasn't that kind of person. She knew that. But there was a first time for everything. *Everything*, her heart echoed.

The silence hovered around them. She felt compelled to fill it. "The weather seems to be warming, doesn't it?"

"Definitely," he replied.

"I think we'll have an early spring."

He smiled, and it tore her heart into pieces, it was so sad. His life had been lonely. He was reaching out to her, and she knew she wouldn't deny him whatever he wanted.

Excitement grew in her. She could feel the telltale glow in her face, her fair skin betraying her attempts at normalcy. She lowered her lashes over her eyes, helpless to contain the yearning in them, yet afraid to expose herself completely.

He reached across the table and touched her temple, then let his finger glide down her cheek. "I'd say a heat wave has already moved in, hmm?"

"Gabe..." She didn't know what she wanted to say. There seemed so much they needed to talk about.

"I like that," he said huskily.

"What?"

"The sound of my name on your lips. When we're alone, perhaps you'll say it again."

"Yes," she said, and heard the promise in the word. He had such power over her. He could make her forget all her resolutions of the past two days when she'd vowed not to delve into his life ever again.

"Such a simple word," he murmured, his mood introspective. "And yet it offers so much." He sighed and frowned. "This shouldn't be happening. Not now."

"Why not?" She felt it was inevitable, like the spinning of the earth, like the movement of planets.

He shook his head. "I can't afford to be vulnerable, not even physically. Wanting you is an ache inside. I go to sleep with it. I wake with it. There's no escape."

She was entranced. This strong, independent man needed her as much as she needed him. She watched him pick up his wineglass, his eyes never leaving her as he drank. His hands were lean, the palms broad, his grip powerful. She knew how gentle they could be when he touched a person.

He was civilized, yet she sensed the primitive man who lived within. She could imagine him coming to this land ten thousand years ago, undaunted by the great distances he'd had to cross.

"What are you thinking?" he asked.

"I've never met a man like you," she said with no thought of hiding the truth. "I'd go with you...to faraway places."

She realized she would. She'd leave her dream and follow his. No, with him, she'd have her dream, too. A house didn't make a home. That was something created by a man and a woman, a haven of love where all dreams could safely grow. That was what she'd felt with her grandparents. That was what she wanted.

The softness in him disappeared like water in a desert. He read her thoughts as if they were written on her face.

"Don't you ever think of protecting yourself?" he demanded, rejecting her and her dreams, rejecting all dreams.

The warm mist surrounding them evaporated. "Yes, of course. If I know what to protect myself from."

He sighed heavily. "I confuse the hell out of you, don't I? Don't feel bad. I do it to myself, too."

"What do you want from me?" she asked, love and anger mixing in equal parts.

His laughter was brief and bitter. "Everything and nothing."

She forced a wry smile. "Now that tells me a lot."

"You've got courage, Whitney Thompson. I'll give you that. If this were another time, another place..."

The withheld promise in the phrase tore at her heart. "What's wrong with the here and now?" she challenged.

"This moment?" he mused. "With no thought to the future or the past? Most women demand a man's soul, not to mention his name and paycheck."

"Well, I know what your paycheck is," she reminded him.

His expression changed, becoming softer. "You know more about me than people who watched me grow up. It's damned unnerving."

She tucked a stray strand of hair behind her ear. "Living in the same house makes a difference. I've seen you grouchy and restless. I've heard you whistle when you're happy. You're neat in your personal habits. You help with the dishes."

"A paragon," he mocked.

"A good man," she quietly insisted.

He sighed.

Their food arrived. She ate, but couldn't recall what it was. When they finished, she refused dessert. So did he. They had coffee. "Ready to go?" he asked when their cups were empty and the bill was paid.

"Yes."

They walked to the truck. The sides of the street were crowded with parked vehicles. People were starting to come to the area in winter as well as summer. Two theaters offered a short winter season, and the college held a series of concerts.

"Ashland is growing," she mused. "It's no longer a college town and farming community. There're so many arts and crafts places now. And specialty boutiques."

Taking the keys, he escorted her to the passenger side of the truck. In a minute, they were on the long drive home.

"Marry a farm boy," her grandmother had once advised, casting a mischievous glance at her husband, who was installing new shelves in the pantry. "They can make or repair anything."

Whitney could still remember the glance the two older people had exchanged. They'd still been lovers, she realized.

She clenched and unclenched her hands on her purse when they turned in the lane to the house. When he stopped the truck near the front steps, he reached over and laid his warm hand over both of hers.

"Nothing's going to happen," he promised.

"That's what I'm afraid of."

He drew a sharp breath. "And if something did?"

She had no answer.

He took her arm when they went up the steps. After opening the front door, he turned to her. "If this were an ordinary date, our first one, I'd leave you here."

"Without a kiss?" She gazed up at him through her lashes.

"I'd have to have that," he murmured, and bent to her.

When their lips met, lightning flashed from the point of contact to every part of her. She thought it was the same for him. She felt his muscles clench when he caught her close.

He made a barely audible sound deep in his throat. Then he pulled her closer, sliding his hands under her parka to caress along her back and down to her hips. His mouth moved sweetly against hers. She loved his taste and the texture of his roaming tongue as he explored her mouth with gentle passion.

She raised her arms and circled his neck, thrusting her fingers into the silky strands of his black hair. The kiss went on and on for mindless minutes.

He lifted his head. "Let's go inside." He pushed the door open and let her enter, then locked it behind them. The house seemed to welcome them with a soft sigh, fragrant with the pine boughs she'd placed on the mantel earlier that day.

Taking her hand, he urged her along the hall when she paused at the base of the steps, not sure where she was supposed to go. She thought, in the swirling mist that had invaded her mind, that it would take a while to become used to being lovers.

"I'll build a fire," he said when they reached her room.

She hung her parka in the closet and dropped her purse on a table. "Good. Shall I make some . . ." She wasn't sure what the proper drink was at a time like this.

"Cocoa would be nice."

She rushed to the kitchen. While the cocoa heated, she leaned against the counter and pressed her cold hands to her hot face.

For a moment, away from the temptation of his arms, she tried to think, to judge what she was doing...what they were going to do. It felt right, but was that the passion of the moment?

The timer beeped. She took the mugs out of the microwave and stirred the steaming cocoa, then tasted it. She decided it was okay. Carrying a mug in each hand, she returned to the bedroom.

Gabe had removed his jacket. His shirtsleeves were rolled back on his muscular arms, the collar open. A few crinkly black hairs showed above the T-shirt he wore. He came to her and took his mug.

She hesitated in choosing a seat, her glance going from the chair to the sofa. He solved the dilemma by sitting on the sofa, moving over so that there was obviously room for her. She sat beside him and stared into the fire now blazing in the grate.

"This is nice," he said. His gesture included them, the room and the fire. He leaned forward, his arms on his thighs, lightly clasping the mug between his knees, his brow furrowed in thought.

After a long silence, she realized her mug was empty. She placed it on the table. He set his aside and turned to her.

She nearly jumped when he placed his arm around her shoulders. "I'm nervous, too," he confessed. "This isn't part of the plan."

He lifted her face to his with a finger under her chin. She licked her lips, ready for his kiss.

His eyes crinkled at the corners when he smiled. "Ready?"

"Yes."

This time, he wasn't gentle. He didn't hurt her—never that—but the hunger was less controlled, more demanding. He kissed her hard, until her lips stung from the fervor. His hands were restless on her. When he slipped them under her sweater, he found the camisole.

"Take it off," he said hoarsely, then spoke in a quieter tone, "Will you?"

She nodded.

He helped her ease the sweater over her head. The ribbon barrette that clipped her hair at her neck came off, too. He laid them aside and pulled the camisole from her slacks. It joined the sweater and ribbon on the coffee table. She hadn't worn a bra. He glanced at the beading of her breasts.

"Your gown, where is it?"

"In the top drawer." She indicated an armoire.

Quickly, he retrieved it. Handing the garment to her, he pulled her up and removed the slacks. She pulled the gown on, self-conscious about her body. Her breasts were small, her ribs showed under the skin and her hips hardly curved at all.

"You're beautiful," he murmured. "When I look at you..." He shook his head as if words failed him.

His reaction always surprised her. She peered at him to see if he was teasing. He looked completely serious. "I think you're beautiful, too."

"That night in the shower...you looked at me and I felt ten feet tall." He stopped her when she started to button the gown. "Leave it open. I want to touch you. Take my shirt off. I want to feel you against me."

In all her twenty-eight years, she'd never undressed a man. The few times she'd tried to go this far, something in her had protested, and she'd known the man wasn't the one.

Gabe Deveraux was. It was that simple.

She lifted her hand to his shirt and slipped the buttons free. She pushed the shirt off his shoulders.

"Here, let me get out of this." He stripped the T-shirt off.

"You'll be cold—"

His laughter stopped her. "I'm burning up."

This time he pulled her onto his lap when he sat on the sofa. He spread her hair around her shoulders and ran his fingers through the heavy waves before cupping her head in his hands and drawing her close. His lips touched hers, and she was consumed by the pure sweetness of it.

He smoothed a hand across her shoulder and down her arm, then to her waist. He ran his fingers under the open edge of her gown, his touch hot on her skin. Then he cradled her breast in his broad palm, covering it fully.

A gasp of pure pleasure was torn from her.

"Touch me like that," he murmured. "You wouldn't believe the times I've thought of your hands on me. Since that night in the shower, I've dreamed of it constantly."

"You should have told me," she scolded breathlessly. "Tell me what you like. Teach me... to please you."

"You please me just by breathing." His breath was warm on her ear as he nibbled there. His fingers formed a rosette on the very tip of her breast and squeezed gently.

Their love play continued. An hour passed. Vaguely she heard the striking of her mantel clock and knew it was late. She wanted more than this touching, wonderful as it was.

"Isn't it time to go to bed?" she suggested.

He lifted his head from her throat. "Yes," he agreed huskily. He lifted her and carried her across the room. He placed her under the covers, then added several logs to the fire to keep the room warm. When he returned, he kicked off his shoes and lay beside her, above the covers, his body partially covering her.

She frowned, not liking the sheet and blankets between them.

"No, leave them," he ordered when she tried to push them aside. "It's safer that way."

"I don't want to be safe," she said, and was immediately shocked at the bold complaint.

Gabe smiled and touched her cheek with his fingertips as the blood ran under her skin. "A brazen hussy of a virgin," he teased in the tenderest voice.

"I... I want..."

"Shh. I know." He sighed regretfully. "But not tonight."

His words made no sense.

He met her gaze. She saw the withdrawal before he said the rest. "I'm not going to make love to you tonight."

She stiffened in disbelief. "Why?"

"It's not a good idea."

"Why not?"

For a second he looked defeated, then he sat up, a smile barely touching his mouth. His fingers trembled when he traced a line across her lips and down her neck. He eased her gown together and began fastening the buttons.

She couldn't believe he was doing this. She pushed her hair behind her ears in an angry gesture.

He caught her hand and kissed the palm. "There are things you don't understand."

"Then tell me!"

"I can't. Not now. There are others involved."

"You don't trust me," she concluded.

He frowned. "I've trusted very few people in my life. It's a lesson not easily forgotten. You need to learn it, too."

He made her sound gullible and naive, like a child who expected all her desires to be granted. But she hadn't asked for promises or commitment. She hadn't made any demands at all.

"I think I could hate you," she whispered.

He looked away and stared into the fire, his expression remote and self-contained. "It would be better if you did."

When he stood, she forced herself to look at him. He stayed there for a second, then sighed, picked up his jacket and shoes, and walked across the room. At the door, he paused. "I may not be here when you wake up in the morning."

She met his dark gaze and nodded as if she understood.

"Goodbye, Irish." He turned and left.

For a long time after he left, she couldn't seem to think. The hunger he incited faded, but nothing could relieve the hunger in her soul. She relived the evening, mulling over every nuance of their "date."

When he'd stopped at the front door and kissed her, she'd thought he had meant to leave then. But one kiss hadn't been enough, not for either of them, so he'd stayed awhile longer.

She pressed her hands to her chest as she remembered his gentle, demanding caresses here in the bedroom. And then there had been the—regret? pity?—in his eyes when he'd left.

Just then, a draft stirred the flames in the fireplace, sending a shower of ash and embers up the chimney. She knew he was gone.

It hit her then—his final words. Not "Good night." Not "I'll see you in the morning." But "Goodbye."

Did goodbye mean forever?

Chapter Ten

Whitney paced in front of the fire. *Something was going to happen that night*. Whatever it was, she was going to be ready. She dressed in thermal underwear, jeans and a light turtleneck sweater with a wool vest. She put on warm socks, then set her boots, parka, gloves and watch cap by the door. She did all this in the dim light of the flickering embers.

Then she ran upstairs.

In the bedroom above hers, she groped over the furniture until she found the binoculars. At the window, she surveyed the outlines of the ranch buildings. If anything was going on at the ranch, it was being done in the light of the moon, which had been full the night before. She couldn't detect any other lights or activity.

She wondered if Gabe was hiding someplace—perhaps in the barn loft. Maybe he was going to try to take pictures of the thieves when they moved the stolen goods. One of those infrared videos would work. Thus he could prove his innocence to the sheriff.

An hour went by. And another. She pulled a padded chair over to the window, fetched a blanket and made herself comfortable. It was going to be a long night.

Picking up the binoculars, she peered through them. To her shock, she could see moving shadows among the motionless shadows of the buildings. Men were there, moving the boxes!

As if electrified, she sat absolutely still and tried to think what she should do. Her first impulse was to call the sheriff, but she thought better of it. If only Gabe had confided something of his plans, then she'd have a better grasp of the situation.

Men! They never thought about the women who loved them when they were off on their little adventures, acting like the heroes in detective novels who caught the crooks and solved the crimes all by themselves.

Sometimes those heroes were shot, she remembered. Books were becoming more realistic nowadays.

She tiptoed down the stairs and put her boots on. She wanted to be ready in case she had to act fast. Upstairs, she propped her elbows on the windowsill—the one Gabe had taken two days to caulk and paint, the binoculars always at his side—and settled down for a long vigil.

It wasn't all that long.

A sudden streak of light brought her upright in the chair. A split second later the sound arrived. *Bang*! She realized two things—someone had fired a gun; Gabe could have been the target.

Two more shots followed in quick succession. Then all was confusion. Lights and noise erupted at the ranch. High-powered spotlights flicked on, illuminating an eighteen-wheeler and the men who had been loading it with the stolen goods.

Through the field glasses, she could see men running... others chasing them...cars arriving...others leaving. It looked like a prime example of mass confusion to her.

She experienced a great desire to head out across the meadow to see what was happening. Common sense urged caution. If she didn't get killed in the shootout, she reasoned, Gabe would surely do it when he saw her. She stayed put.

Finally, after what seemed like hours, the commotion stopped. Flashing blue lights along the road indicated more police arriving. She heard the baying of hounds and realized the police had brought in tracking dogs. Some of the thieves must have gotten away.

Where was Gabe in all this?

Two more hours passed before things seemed to calm down and cars began to leave. At dawn, there were only two vehicles left. She wished her binoculars were strong enough for her to identify the men, but they were only moving blobs in the landscape. All seemed calm now.

She went downstairs and put on a full pot of strong coffee. She hesitated, then started the waffle iron to heating. She'd poured the first cup of batter onto the iron when she heard the front door open and close.

She felt as if her chest had been invaded by a lead weight. It was very hard to breathe all at once. "Coffee's ready," she called out. She sounded almost normal.

Gabe appeared at the kitchen door. He leaned against it, looking so weary, she nearly went to him.

"Have a seat," she said, hiding her concern. She wouldn't ask questions, not a one. If he wanted to tell her anything, he would volunteer it. "Breakfast will be ready in a few minutes."

She put sausage in the microwave, then poured a mug of coffee and refilled her own. She carried the coffee to the table. Gabe walked over. Shrugging out of his dark parka, he laid it over the chair back before sitting down.

After placing the mug on the table, she poured two glasses of orange juice and took those over. Then she set the table. It was only when these chores were completed that she dared to really look at him.

"You've been hurt!" she exclaimed. She bent over and stared at the bruise forming high on his cheekbone.

"It's nothing."

He shied away when she would have touched him. Dropping her hand as if stung, she went to the refrigerator and brought him an ice cube after wrapping it in a paper towel. He took it without a word.

She moved about the kitchen, her mind focused on the tasks at hand while questions roiled within her.

"Better get it off your chest," he invited.

His mocking humor infuriated her already lacerated senses. "You could have been killed. I saw the lights...there were shots. The police... the dogs... I was so worried..." She trailed into silence at his harsh laugh.

"I'm surprised you didn't dash right into the thick of things."

His sardonic manner cut deep. She felt the tears rise, and pushed them back with an effort. "I thought of it."

Their eyes met; hers defiant, his searching. He was wary, she realized, but he was interested in her reactions. She clamped her mouth shut, determined not to give him cause to accuse her of wearing her heart on her sleeve.

He drank the steaming coffee, his lean, hard body slumped in his chair like a man who'd returned home after a long, hard trip.

When the waffles and sausage were done, she loaded up their plates and took a seat opposite him at the small table.

"That looks good," he said. Again he watched her.

She said nothing.

Picking up her fork, she began to eat. Her appetite wasn't much, but Gabe ate every bite, quickly and efficiently cleaning his plate. She rinsed and stacked the dishes in the dishwasher, then leaned against the counter and sipped her coffee.

He did the same. It seemed they were at a standoff. Neither had anything to say.

"Did you sleep any last night?" he asked.

She shook her head.

"It's an odd feeling," he mused, "to know someone gives a damn." A smile flitted over his face and was gone.

She stared into the swirls of steam rising from her mug and hoped he'd continue that thought and confide in her. When he didn't, she sighed. Her spirits dipped to their lowest.

The sound of a car engine signaled the end of their privacy. She went to the living room to see who was calling at—the wall clock pointed to five minutes before seven. Lots of people up early that day, it seemed.

The car turned out to be a utility truck that belonged to the sheriff. He got out and climbed the steps to the front porch. She opened the door. "Come in," she invited, her smile confident, her heart quaking. "The coffee's ready."

"Good. I hope it's hot and strong."

"It is," Gabe said from the kitchen doorway.

Sheriff Macklin headed in that direction, his stride long and purposeful, his gun, black and lethal, strapped around his lean waist. He was as tall and as big as Gabe.

Whitney followed the men. She poured a mug of coffee for the law officer and willed her hand not to tremble when she placed the mug on the table in front of him. She had to appear casual, as if she didn't suspect anything was wrong.

Macklin flicked her a glance, murmured his thanks, then turned his gaze back to Gabe. He didn't smile. Neither did he appear in any great hurry as he sipped the hot coffee. He looked as tired as Gabe, she noted with a stir of sympathy. However, her concern was for Gabe at the moment.

He didn't seem worried at all. Instead he appeared almost casual. He pushed his chair back so he could stretch his long, muscular legs to the side and cross them at the ankles, covering a yawn as he did. He took a drink of coffee and waited with total outward composure for the sheriff to begin.

She leaned against the counter and forced herself not to pace while she mentally searched for a way to protect Gabe from his own folly in going to the ranch. She could say she'd heard a noise and had awakened him...that she'd asked him to go check it out... that neither of them had suspected the stolen goods were in the barn. She could say he hadn't been near the Deveraux ranch the entire time he'd worked for her.

Who in his right mind would believe that Gabe had been next door to his place and not been interested enough to look it over?

She glanced at the sheriff. He didn't look stupid. In fact, his eyes were alert and wary, in spite of the lines of fatigue on his face. She tried to think of something... *anything*...

The ticking of the clock was the only sound in the house for a minute that lasted an eternity.

"Well, first the bad news," Shane Macklin said. The corners of his mouth turned up in a wry twist.

Whitney swallowed, then took a deep breath. Gabe shot her a glance. She clamped her mouth shut.

"One of the crooks got away," the sheriff continued.

Whitney cast a frantic glance at Gabe. He sat there like a rock. He wasn't going to say a word in his defense. She knew him and his damnable male pride. He'd let his father beat him rather than plead his case.

Macklin put the mug on the table, his manner deceptively casual. "The dogs tracked a set of prints this way—"

"It wasn't Gabe."

Whitney raised her chin and stood her ground. She couldn't bear to see Gabe falsely accused and arrested. She knew he was innocent. His only crime had been in not confiding his plans to someone who could vouch for his honesty. She would have to do it for him.

The two men looked at her, then each other, then back at her. Gabe frowned ominously.

She refused to be daunted. There was a time to make a brave, solitary stand, but this wasn't it. He needed an ally. She didn't know why he couldn't see that. Proud, stubborn loner. She would be his friend whether he wanted one or not.

"Well," the sheriff drawled, an odd smile playing about his mouth, "the footprints looked similar." He looked at her and waited to see what she would say to this indisputable proof.

"They weren't." Whitney licked her lips and took the final plunge. "He wasn't out of the house last night."

Gabe stared out the window, so still he could have been carved in stone. He wasn't going to utter a word in his defense. The sheriff seemed interested in her story, but skeptical of its truth. Desperation seized her.

"He was here," she insisted, then threw in the clincher, "with me." She felt the telltale blood rise to her face and tried to stop it by force of will.

"Hmm," the sheriff said. He clearly didn't believe her. In fact, he was almost laughing.

"All night," she added firmly.

The sheriff smiled, his eyes so full of amused admiration that it startled her. She tried to think of how to convince him.

"In... in my bed," she said in case there was any doubt in anyone's mind about what she meant.

Gabe choked on his coffee.

When she dared glance at him, she saw him put a hand over his eyes. His face went a surprising shade of barn red.

The law officer chuckled and shook his head. "Damn," he said in an envious tone to Gabe, "if I ever found a woman like that, I'd grab her with both hands."

Gabe snorted and dropped his hand. "Strangle her would be more like it," he muttered, but he didn't sound angry.

Whitney couldn't figure out what was going on. The men seemed to know something she didn't. The feeling she'd made a ghastly mistake took root. She clutched the coffee mug in a death grip.

"I hate to dispute a lady's word," Shane Macklin said kindly, "but Gabe was with me at least half of the night."

"With you?" she repeated. Gabe had been with the sheriff? The implication hit her, and she slumped with relief. "Then you know he's not a crook?" she inquired anxiously.

"Right. He's one of the good guys." He chuckled again.

She realized she had made a total fool of herself with her lie about Gabe being with her *in her bed* all night. No wonder he'd wanted to strangle her before she embarrassed him further. A fresh tide of heat beat its way up her neck. It was one of those times when a person wished the floor would open under them.

Macklin stood and stretched. "Thanks for the coffee. Maybe I'll stay awake long enough to get to the office. I'll need your report...as soon as you can get in," he told Gabe with a smiling glance at Whitney. "We should have word on the thieves soon."

"I know who one of them was," Gabe spoke up. "He was in high school when I was. We used to pal around some."

"I recognized him." A hardness entered Macklin's eyes. "I suspect he's been operating in the state for a long time by moving around when things get too hot in one place. He was a thief in high school, too, but it was never proven."

"I'd suspected as much."

Whitney realized Gabe's friend was the one who'd framed him years ago. Gabe had known. Another betrayal of trust. No wonder he was wary of any ties whatsoever.

"Nice seeing you, Miss Thompson." The lawman nodded to her as he headed for the door. She followed him.

"Please, call me Whitney. Thank you for coming by."

She stood in the open door when he went out, and wondered if she should apologize for lying to him, but when he smiled and waved, she smiled politely and waved back.

When she turned, Gabe was standing in the kitchen doorway, one hand propped on the frame, the other tucked into his back pocket.

Her composure wavered at the dark, brooding expression in his eyes. He probably wished he'd never laid eyes on her.

She decided she'd better get the confrontation over. "It seems I butted in again," she said, starting out bravely enough. "I thought... I was wrong, of course... but I was afraid..."

He didn't help at all, but stared at her the entire time she tried to explain, rattling her completely. She stopped.

"Were you afraid I was one of the thieves?" he asked, his tone cold and hard... so hard. He turned and walked into the kitchen without waiting for an answer.

She was shocked at his interpretation of her actions. "Of course not!" She followed him. "I was afraid the sheriff thought you were, though. I knew you weren't—"

"How?" he broke in. "How did you know that?" He paced the floor like a restless panther, dark and dangerous and yet so very desirable to her.

"I—" She tried to think of some clue he'd let slip. "Well, it seemed to me, since you were hurt when I found you... I mean, if you'd been one of the gang, you wouldn't have had to hide from them, would you?"

She took up her former position against the counter and sipped at the lukewarm coffee without tasting it. The mug formed an effective shield for her hands and lips, both of which had a tendency to tremble when he looked at her.

He stopped pacing and stood a short distance away. She wished he'd take her in his arms and comfort her. She felt the need for some tenderness after the harrowing night, plus having to deal with the law on top of everything else.

"Didn't you ever hear of a falling out among thieves?" he said in answer to her question, the sardonic humor surfacing.

She realized he used it to close people out. "You're not a thief."

Except maybe of hearts. She held the mug tighter as the ache inside deepened. She wished he would either go and let her be miserable in peace or make love to her until she basked in the warmth of his passion and forgot there was a tomorrow... and that he was going to leave.

"Only you and the police believe that at the present," he told her. "The rest of the valley thinks differently."

"The rest of the valley is wrong."

He studied her, as if trying to decide what to do. For a moment, gazing into his eyes, she saw turmoil, as if he engaged in a war with himself. For a second, she recognized the stark need of one human for another. She saw the loneliness he'd lived with for years, the yearning he denied even to himself.

Slowly, carefully, she opened herself to his inspection, letting him see into the farthest recesses where her dreams lived out their lonely existence. She let him see the love she had for him, the deep need that drove her to take his side against all reason. She let him see her soul. It wasn't enough.

He blinked, and the moment was gone. "This isn't part of the plan," he protested in a low growl.

"Plans change," she countered softly, knowing it was useless. "Dreams grow into new ones." But, if he had dreams, she evidently wasn't part of them.

"I have to go to town," he said.

She nodded. "You can take the truck."

He reached out so suddenly, she jumped. He smoothed back the hair at her temple, his eyes so fierce, so blazing, she wondered what had stirred his temper. Oddly, his tone was gentle. "I'll be back as soon as I can. Then we'll talk."

"Shall I go with you?"

"I think Macklin can defend me against Mrs. Tall and the town gossips, if you're worried about them."

"Well, I..." She stopped when he smiled, a rueful smile, but a real one. "Oh, you're teasing me."

She realized he was no longer very far from her. In fact, he was very close, so close she was enclosed in his body heat. It radiated over her like a benign sun, soaking her in his warmth, his masculine strength, the powerful tenderness she knew was in him.

He touched her cheek, her lips. "You're a temptation no man should have to resist." He sighed. "But there are other things that have to be said."

"Gabe..."

All at once, she knew he wouldn't leave without making love to her. It was a certainty borne out by the hunger in his eyes. When she would have touched him, he stepped out of reach.

"Not now. Not yet," he said raggedly. His chest lifted in a quick breath. "I want you...probably more than you can imagine, but you have to know what you're getting into...if you get involved with me."

She realized he would stay awhile longer. It didn't matter how long. They would have time together. "Hurry," she said.

"We're both too tired to cope with unbridled passion at the present." Gabe watched the thought bring pleasure to her eyes and a blush to her cheeks. "It's probably best that you have some time to think. Sleep for a couple of hours, if you can."

"Only with you," she told him.

"Neither of us would sleep." He touched her under her chin and left her, another of his rare smiles on his face.

When he had left, she curled into the easy chair in her room and fell asleep at once.

A hand on her shoulder woke her hours later.

"Ready to go to town?" Gabe asked. "We're invited to the resort for dinner. Everyone wants to know about the shootout."

She figured everyone in town knew of her lie about Gabe being with her all night. She wasn't ready to face the ridicule yet. "You go," she said. "I think I'll stay here. I don't feel like dressing up."

"You look fine." He hesitated. "I need to talk to Rafe. There are things I want you to hear."

Put that way, how could she refuse? "Five minutes," she requested.

He nodded and left her.

She combed her hair, pinned it back with combs over her temples, and added lipstick.

They left shortly, Gabe at the wheel while she watched the scenery flash by. "Spring is creeping upon us," she commented at one point. "The willow buds are swelling."

"Yeah. I noticed some birds flying in."

"Mr. Peters will probably be back soon. He'll be surprised to find the work done." She smiled in satisfaction. When Gabe glanced at her, she tingled all over.

Whatever he wanted her to hear, she knew it would make no difference in her feelings for him. He was a good person. Maybe he'd gotten into trouble in the past—he may even have been in prison as Mrs. Tall had suggested—but he was an honorable man. His actions with her proved it.

"By the way, they tracked the other man, the one who got away, up the creek toward the resort. He was caught near there."

"Good," she said.

Gabe gave her another penetrating glance, then concentrated on the road. She wished the evening were over. She wanted to be alone with him.

At the resort, he parked in the drive of a town house, the last unit in a building set high on the hillside. Other buildings were attractively arranged on the sloping terrain.

"Is this where you worked?" she asked.

He found this humorous. "Yes." Ignoring the front door, he led her around to a set of steps in the back.

Rafe Barrett was there to open the door before they knocked. They entered the kitchen. "Come in. Dinner is almost done," he announced. "I cooked. Genny's doing the taste test." He took their coats and hung them over a newel post. Oak stairs led upward to the second story of the house.

His fiancée smiled from across the room. "Here. See if this has enough salt." She handed the spoon to Whitney.

Whitney tasted the sauce. "It's fine."

"Good. Everything is ready. Shall we go into the den?"

They had wine and appetizers in a comfortable room off a central atrium. "I feel terribly disloyal to my grandmother's Victorian, but I really like your home," Whitney told them.

After the meal, Genny gave her a tour of the house.

"You should think about putting in a hot tub," Genny said with a secretive smile. "It's really nice."

"That sounds like an understatement." Whitney's eyes met Genny's. They smiled as understanding flared between them. Whitney realized the other woman knew and approved of her feelings for Gabe. It gave her a warm feeling of friendship.

The men were deep in discussion regarding the past three months. As she listened, she realized Gabe was much more than a handyman, as other times and places were mentioned.

Whitney had a feeling the other three knew lots of things that she didn't know... just like the sheriff and Gabe did.

"Well, another case solved by Special Agent Deveraux," Genny announced when the talk ended.

Whitney turned startled eyes on Gabe.

"Uh-oh, I think I spoke out of turn," Genny murmured.

Gabe give Genny a resigned glance, then he looked at Whitney, clearly expecting a question. But she couldn't think of where to start. She simply stared at him, feeling betrayed and left out.

"I think we'd better go," he announced, standing and drawing her up with him. "It's been a long day."

Whitney thanked the couple for dinner and a lovely evening. "They were very nice," she said softly when they were on their way.

"Yes. Rafe and I worked together for several years in Europe and the Mideast."

"Oh." She hesitated, then asked, "So he was an agent, too?"

"Chief Information Officer was his title."

"And yours?"

He turned from the dark ribbon of road and gave her a level glance. "Head of Covert Intelligence."

"I see." Whitney pondered this on the way home, her heart heavy. So many things were clear now. She understood why Gabe was restless. He had an exciting job that involved him in worldwide adventures. How very, very foolish she'd been to think he might be tempted to stay with her in her bed-and-breakfast inn.

Gabe followed Whitney down the hall at the old Victorian mansion. He knew the place from top to bottom. He looked at the work the two of them had accomplished during the time he'd been there. It was a sturdy house, meant to hold generations of a family. An odd sensation clutched at his insides.

He went to the fireplace, added kindling and built up the fire from the embers. Whitney made cocoa.

It was almost a tradition with them, he thought, taking the tray when she returned and placing it on the coffee table. Whitney sat in the easy chair.

Gabe watched her, the hunger growing in him. He needed her. He admitted it. She was like the sun, thawing out his heart in the springtime of her smile...her love. He didn't know what to do about her. There was still the town and his dislike of it. She handed him a cup of steaming chocolate. He sipped it.

"Now you see the problem," he finally said.

"What problem?"

Her glance was so guileless, he almost believed she was that innocent. Maybe she was.

He was deliberately blunt. If she got involved with him for the short time he intended to stay, she'd have to know what she faced. He told her of his life, his association with gun runners, thieves, hired killers. "Life could be dangerous if any of them decided to come gunning for me like they did for Rafe and Genny."

"I'd take that chance," she said quietly, her gaze focused on some internal horizon as if she saw into the future, "for the man I loved. Any woman would."

An invisible hand seized his throat. For a second he couldn't breathe.

Dauntless. It was the only word for her. Brave. Unafraid. *Foolish*. He'd have to make her see sense where they were concerned. "Well, I'm not asking you to."

Again she surprised him. She didn't get mad or weepy. She only smiled in a sad, tender way. "I know."

He felt as if a giant hand were squeezing his heart. He swallowed the words that rushed to his throat and fought the need to take her in his arms and comfort her for all the wrongs she'd ever suffered. *Ah, Irish . . .*

"I'll be leaving soon." He waited, realizing he wanted a protest from her, some sign that she wouldn't let him go without an argument. He *wanted* her to argue with him.

So he could leave in anger instead of misery?

"Gabe . . ."

He waited, wary of the way he felt, the way she made him feel. "What?" he prodded when she failed to speak.

"About when the sheriff came . . . about what I said . . ."

A knot formed in his throat as he remembered how she'd stepped in and lied for him. *Lied. For him*. She'd taken his side without a thought for herself or her reputation in the community where she was trying to establish her life . . . her dream. He nodded to show he knew which time she meant.

"I'm sorry I embarrassed you. I thought I was helping—"

"You're what?"

She clutched the cup until her knuckles went white. "I didn't know, of course, that you'd been with the sheriff . . . If you'd told me . . ." Her face reddened. "Well, that doesn't matter. Anyway, I'm terribly sorry. You were right to be angry. You should have strangled me." She smiled. It was the bravest thing he ever saw.

"You didn't embarrass me," he murmured past the ache in his throat. "No one had ever done what you did for me in my entire life. No one has ever believed in me like that. I wanted to throw myself on the floor and kiss your feet." He gave a snort of laughter. "I probably would have, except I was afraid I wouldn't be able to stop there. I wanted all of you."

She raised her head, startled by his confession. He let her look into his eyes . . . into his soul. If she wanted him . . . if she'd take him, he'd stay . . . No, he had to think of her, of her future. He closed his heart on his desires and tried to think only of her.

"You can have . . . everything," she offered, an endearing shyness entering her tone. She gave him a smiling glance, then calmly drank her chocolate. Only the tremor in her fingers gave her away.

"Irish," he began in frustration. The need ate at him. He had only to reach out and take her. She'd come to him. She'd give him peace and warmth and happiness. What would he give her? What if he disappointed her . . . ?

While this argument went on inside him, she set the cup aside, rose and faced him. "I don't care about possible danger. A person can get eaten by a bear, but that doesn't stop people from going into the woods. I want you to stay, but if you can't live here, then I'll go with you, wherever you go. If you'll let me."

He felt as if his heart had burst wide open. He hurt inside. A home . . . with her. She was offering her life, her soul. But there was her life to think of . . . What if she wasn't happy with him . . . ?

"I love you," she said softly.

Once the words were said, he couldn't ignore them. They danced in the air between them, a golden promise of all the good things in life. He had only to reach out . . .

"God," he muttered, rubbing a hand over his face. His skull felt too little to hold his thoughts. "That first time, when I was hurt . . . when I opened my eyes and stared into the bluest eyes I'd ever seen, I felt like I was drowning." He gave a brief laugh. "I still do." *Going once . . . going twice . . .*

She didn't look away from his tortured gaze, but remained silent, as if she sensed the struggle going on in him. He saw the pain in her eyes and knew he couldn't bear for her to be hurt, not even for her own good. She thought he didn't love her.

"Gone," he said, defeated by her steadfast love and his need for her. He knew he was being selfish—

"Are you staying?" she asked quietly.

"If you want me to."

"If...well, of course I want you to. I've wanted it from the very first moment I saw you."

The last fragments of wall came tumbling down. His heart was open, exposed, vulnerable. He tried to speak lightly. "Yeah, when I was laid out in the snow with my foot in a trap. A prize catch."

"Yes, even then, but before that, too. I'd watched you through my binoculars for a week."

He wasn't surprised. "I knew I was being watched."

"When I brought you home, I thought..." The glow seeped into her cheeks.

He loved her skin. It betrayed her every emotion. Soon she'd be rosy all over. He'd make love to her... He tamped down the surge of desire. As soon as they were married. Total commitment, that was the very least she deserved.

"What?" he demanded, pushing close. "What did you think?"

"Well, I found you. It seemed you should belong to me."

"Finders keepers?"

"Yes," she said.

He knelt in front of her. She touched his hair, inviting him closer. He leaned forward, pressing his face into the warmth of her body. Moving back, she slipped down until she, too, was on her knees. She reached for him, wanting his kiss.

He cupped her face in his broad hands. "Will you share your dreams with me?" he asked in a husky voice. "Are they big enough to include another?" He stopped and looked at her.

"Yes," she whispered. "Oh, yes. I have dreams enough. For us, for our future, for a lifetime." She leaned against him and linked her arms around his neck.

He'd never known such trust. He kissed her, softly and with restraint. She wanted more. She pressed against him.

"Not yet," he told her huskily. "I have to resign and make arrangements—"

"No. No more plans," she said, a stubborn edge to the words. "I want you now."

"We have to give the town a chance to calm down after all the excitement and accept who I am and that I'm going to stay. Rafe and the sheriff can vouch for me—"

"You don't need anyone to vouch for you," she stated indignantly. "If the town can't see how wonderful you are, then it's their loss."

He gazed at her. The hunger blazed within. He'd tried to be honorable, to consider her future, but he knew he couldn't give her up. It was too much to ask of a man. She was his—his gift from life. He didn't deserve her, but she didn't seem to care. She loved him, and she was willing to take her chances.

Good enough.

"I can't fight both of us," he said unsteadily. "Marry me, Irish. It will be the ultimate test of your faith."

"It's no test at all. I knew you were a good man from the moment we met." She sighed happily.

"How?" He tried to understand her faith.

"My grandmother told me to marry a farm boy. She said they were the best."

He lifted her and settled on the sofa, her on his lap. "A wise woman," he murmured, then he kissed her.

Chapter Eleven

Whitney and Gabe walked hand in hand across the meadow. At the barbed-wire fence, he held the upper strand while she climbed through. She did the same for him. They resumed their journey.

A light snow fell around them, the flakes so big they looked like feathers sifting down from the sky. One lit on her nose. She laughed and shook it off.

Gabe stopped and looked at her.

She paused and watched the emotions skim through his eyes. They stood on his land, a place that held unhappy memories for him. She wondered about the happy ones. "I can imagine you as a boy, running across this very meadow, sneaking through the fence and heading for the best fishing hole."

He peered over the fields toward the creek, which was white with a covering of ice and snow except in a couple of deep places. "I used to do that," he said.

She said nothing, letting his memories take over. He took her hand and they resumed walking.

"I remember my first horse," he said. "A small mare, almost as little as a pony. I wanted a big horse... like my dad's."

"Um," she said, gently encouraging the line of thought.

During the three weeks of their marriage, she'd told him of her childhood, of her mother's restless search for some illusive dream of love that didn't exist. She'd explained her view of her grandparents' marriage—a thing they'd worked at with humor and lots of indulgence for each other's foibles. Gently she'd urged him to tell of his early years.

It had been hard for him, but he'd opened up to her. He spoke of his youth when each day had seemed so full of promise.

"The life on a ranch or farm," he'd mused. "A continuous cycle of birth and death. Sometimes you feel so close to nature, to the very breath of life. At others, it seems to go against you and you watch your stock die in a blizzard... It reminds you that there are forces bigger than you in the world."

At night, talking after they'd made wonderful, fulfilling love, she'd learned of his mother's death and how it had left an emptiness inside. "My father must have felt it, too. He'd always been a quiet man. After that, he became grim."

When Gabe had told her this, he'd raised up on his elbow and gazed down at her. The firelight had flickered over his dark, golden skin, enthralling her with all the mysterious maleness he possessed. He was once again the ancient tracker she'd first seen through her field glasses—a wanderer in search of home, his gaze attuned to faraway places.

Now she was included in that vista. When she looked into his eyes, she saw herself reflected there, in his dreams, in his heart. She squeezed his hand and lifted her face to the snowy sky, feeling so full of life she thought she might burst.

"Are you as happy as you look?" he murmured.

"Oh, yes, my love, I am. I truly am." She laughed and snuggled close to his side.

Together they walked across his land—the inheritance he hadn't wanted—and entered the iron gate to the little cemetery.

He waited while she read all the names on the tombstones, then he stopped in front of his parents' graves. Whitney remained silent while he contemplated the names and dates.

After several minutes he sighed. "I never understood my father," he said slowly. "He kept himself too closed off."

She nodded when Gabe looked at her.

"I did the same. Maybe it was pride. Maybe we both thought it was a weakness to display any need. I hope to do better by my son, to teach him it's all right to love and to show it."

Gabe pulled her into his arms, his chest to her back so they could look across the land to the mountains. He felt the strength in her slender frame. She was a woman who could hold her own. He'd been lucky.

"I love you, Irish," he said in a low, passionate voice, his cheek resting against her temple. "You're my good-luck piece. My redheaded charm."

His for life.

* * * * *

CELEBRATION 1000! FREE GIFT OFFER

ORDER INFORMATION:

To receive your free AUSTRIAN CRYSTAL BRACELET, send four original proof-of-purchase coupons from any SILHOUETTE ROMANCE™ title published in April through July 1994 with the Free Gift Certificate completed, plus $2.75 for postage and handling (check or money order—please do not send cash) payable to Silhouette Books CELEBRATION 1000! Offer. Hurry! Quantities are limited.

FREE GIFT CERTIFICATE 093 KBM

Name:____________________

Address:____________________

City:__________ State/Prov.:__________ Zip/Postal:__________

Account #:____________________

Mail this certificate, four proofs-of-purchase and check or money order to CELEBRATION 1000! Offer, Silhouette Books, 3010 Walden Avenue, P.O. Box 9048, Buffalo, NY 14269-9048 *or* P.O. Box 623, Fort Erie, Ontario L2A 5X3. Please allow 4-6 weeks for delivery. Offer expires August 31, 1994.

PLUS

Every time you submit a completed certificate with the correct number of proofs-of-purchase, you are automatically entered in our CELEBRATION 1000! SWEEPSTAKES to win the GRAND PRIZE OF $1000 CASH! PLUS, 1000 runner-up prizes of a FREE Silhouette Romance™, autographed by one of CELEBRATION 1000!'s special featured authors, will be awarded. No purchase or obligation necessary to enter. See below for alternate means of entry and how to obtain complete sweepstakes rules.

CELEBRATION 1000! SWEEPSTAKES
NO PURCHASE OR OBLIGATION NECESSARY TO ENTER

You may enter the sweepstakes without taking advantage of the CELEBRATION 1000! FREE GIFT OFFER by hand-printing on a 3" x 5" card (mechanical reproductions are not acceptable) your name and address and mailing it to: CELEBRATION 1000! Sweepstakes, P.O. Box 9048, Buffalo, NY 14269-9048 *or* P.O. Box 623, Fort Erie, Ontario L2A 5X3. Limit: one entry per envelope. Entries must be sent via First Class mail and be received no later than August 31, 1994. No liability is assumed for lost, late or misdirected mail.

Sweepstakes is open to residents of the U.S. (except Puerto Rico) and Canada, 18 years of age or older. All federal, state, provincial, municipal and local laws apply. Offer void wherever prohibited by law. Odds of winning dependent on the number of entries received. For complete rules, send a self-addressed, stamped envelope to: CELEBRATION 1000!-6932 Rules, P.O. Box 4200, Blair, NE 68009.

ONE PROOF OF PURCHASE

093KBM

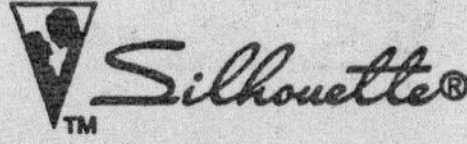

BABY BLESSED
Debbie Macomber

Molly Larabee didn't expect her reunion with estranged husband Jordan to be quite so explosive. Their tumultuous past was filled with memories of tragedy—and love. Rekindling familiar passions left Molly with an unexpected blessing...and suddenly a future with Jordan was again worth fighting for!

Don't miss Debbie Macomber's fiftieth book, BABY BLESSED, available in July!

She's friend, wife, mother—she's you! And beside each **Special Woman** stands a wonderfully *special* man. It's a celebration of our heroines—and the men who become part of their lives.

TSW794

INDULGE A LITTLE 6947 SWEEPSTAKES
NO PURCHASE NECESSARY

HERE'S HOW THE SWEEPSTAKES WORKS:
The Harlequin Reader Service shipments for January, February and March 1994 will contain, respectively, coupons for entry into three prize drawings: a trip for two to San Francisco, an Alaskan cruise for two and a trip for two to Hawaii. To be eligible for any drawing using an Entry Coupon, simply complete and mail according to directions.

There is no obligation to continue as a Reader Service subscriber to enter and be eligible for any prize drawing. You may also enter any drawing by hand printing your name and address on a 3" x 5" card and the destination of the prize you wish that entry to be considered for (i.e., San Francisco trip, Alaskan cruise or Hawaiian trip). Send your 3" x 5" entries to: Indulge a Little 6947 Sweepstakes, c/o Prize Destination you wish that entry to be considered for, P.O. Box 1315, Buffalo, NY 14269-1315, U.S.A. or Indulge a Little 6947 Sweepstakes, P.O. Box 610, Fort Erie, Ontario L2A 5X3, Canada.

To be eligible for the San Francisco trip, entries must be received by 4/30/94; for the Alaskan cruise, 5/31/94; and the Hawaiian trip, 6/30/94. No responsibility is assumed for lost, late or misdirected mail. Sweepstakes open to residents of the U.S. (except Puerto Rico) and Canada, 18 years of age or older. All applicable laws and regulations apply. Sweepstakes void wherever prohibited.

For a copy of the Official Rules, send a self-addressed, stamped envelope (WA residents need not affix return postage) to: Indulge a Little 6947 Rules, P.O. Box 4631, Blair, NE 68009, U.S.A.

INDR93

INDULGE A LITTLE 6947 SWEEPSTAKES
NO PURCHASE NECESSARY

HERE'S HOW THE SWEEPSTAKES WORKS:
The Harlequin Reader Service shipments for January, February and March 1994 will contain, respectively, coupons for entry into three prize drawings: a trip for two to San Francisco, an Alaskan cruise for two and a trip for two to Hawaii. To be eligible for any drawing using an Entry Coupon, simply complete and mail according to directions.

There is no obligation to continue as a Reader Service subscriber to enter and be eligible for any prize drawing. You may also enter any drawing by hand printing your name and address on a 3" x 5" card and the destination of the prize you wish that entry to be considered for (i.e., San Francisco trip, Alaskan cruise or Hawaiian trip). Send your 3" x 5" entries to: Indulge a Little 6947 Sweepstakes, c/o Prize Destination you wish that entry to be considered for, P.O. Box 1315, Buffalo, NY 14269-1315, U.S.A. or Indulge a Little 6947 Sweepstakes, P.O. Box 610, Fort Erie, Ontario L2A 5X3, Canada.

To be eligible for the San Francisco trip, entries must be received by 4/30/94; for the Alaskan cruise, 5/31/94; and the Hawaiian trip, 6/30/94. No responsibility is assumed for lost, late or misdirected mail. Sweepstakes open to residents of the U.S. (except Puerto Rico) and Canada, 18 years of age or older. All applicable laws and regulations apply. Sweepstakes void wherever prohibited.

For a copy of the Official Rules, send a self-addressed, stamped envelope (WA residents need not affix return postage) to: Indulge a Little 6947 Rules, P.O. Box 4631, Blair, NE 68009, U.S.A.

INDR93

INDULGE A LITTLE
SWEEPSTAKES

OFFICIAL ENTRY COUPON

This entry must be received by: JUNE 30, 1994
This month's winner will be notified by: JULY 15, 1994
Trip must be taken between: AUGUST 31, 1994-AUGUST 31, 1995

YES, I want to win the 3-Island Hawaiian vacation for two. I understand that the prize includes round-trip airfare, first-class hotels and pocket money as revealed on the "wallet" scratch-off card.

Name____

Address ________________________ Apt. ______________

City____

State/Prov.__________________ Zip/Postal Code______________

Daytime phone number______________________________
(Area Code)

Account #____________________________________

Return entries with invoice in envelope provided. Each book in this shipment has two entry coupons—and the more coupons you enter, the better your chances of winning!

 MONTH3

INDULGE A LITTLE
SWEEPSTAKES

OFFICIAL ENTRY COUPON

This entry must be received by: JUNE 30, 1994
This month's winner will be notified by: JULY 15, 1994
Trip must be taken between: AUGUST 31, 1994-AUGUST 31, 1995

YES, I want to win the 3-Island Hawaiian vacation for two. I understand that the prize includes round-trip airfare, first-class hotels and pocket money as revealed on the "wallet" scratch-off card.

Name____

Address ________________________ Apt. ______________

City____

State/Prov.__________________ Zip/Postal Code______________

Daytime phone number______________________________
(Area Code)

Account #____________________________________

Return entries with invoice in envelope provided. Each book in this shipment has two entry coupons—and the more coupons you enter, the better your chances of winning!

© 1993 HARLEQUIN ENTERPRISES LTD. MONTH3